Confessions of a Surrogate for Celebrities

Also by **Anne Drea**

Confessions of a Surrogate for Celebrities

By Anne Drea

Anne Drea

ISBN: 978-0-9904430-1-8.

Confessions of a Surrogate for Celebrities

By Anne Drea

Anne Drea

Preface

This is not your ordinary novel. As you read, you will notice two distinct differences. One, unlike other memoir-type novels, this one is purposely missing identifying information, and two, is thus shorter than the ordinary novel. These distinctions are important to note.

The reason this novel is missing identifying information is because, in many cases, I have had to sign an NDA which limits, and in some cases restricts, my ability to disclose certain facts and figures. An NDA is a Nondisclosure Agreement which contractually binds and obligates me to keep certain information a secret.

The NDAs I've signed, and in some cases had my clients sign, prohibits the disclosing of the particulars of the surrogacy arrangements. Specifically, the NDAs prevent me from disclosing names, dates, times, and places.

So how am I able to tell this story? I am able to tell this story by keeping the specific information vague. For example, instead of referring to my celebrity clients by their names, I refer to them using indicators related to their occupation or status, or some other vaguely identifying information. For example, some of the "names" I use include: "The Singer" or "The Actress". Also, instead of saying a specific date, such as March 16, 2011, I'll say "six months later." Additionally, instead of saying we met at one o'clock in the afternoon, I'll simply say we met in the afternoon. And lastly, instead of naming specific restaurants, I'll say we went to eat at a restaurant.

The second distinction is that this story is shorter than an ordinary novel. One might even call it a novella. The reason it is shorter is because it is not an ordinary novel. This is my story. I am not seeking fame, glory, or money; I seek only to tell my story, to disclose the secrets of this seemingly glamorous profession and to confess the ugly truth.

For me, this story is not simply about entertaining my audience; it is also about providing information. The information I provide is solely about my experience being a celebrity surrogate. I will not bore you with unnecessary background information. I will not list my likes and dislikes. I will not detract from the substance of this story by giving you minute and unimportant details.

What I will give you is my background as it relates to becoming a celebrity surrogate, some of the likes and dislikes of my celebrity clients, and enough detail to allow you, the audience, an opportunity to guess at whom I might be referring.

Note that as previously mentioned, the NDA's I have signed do not allow me to reveal too much in the way of specifics, but I believe what information I do provide will allow for some interesting discussions around the water cooler.

My hope is that you will find this information to be succinct and to the point. I seek to tell you what is necessary to shatter the larger-than-life illusion many people have of celebrities. They are regular people, just like the rest of us, but often with more secrets.

The fact that they can spend more money hiding their secrets – or making us believe that we don't know what we know that we know, or we didn't see what we know that we saw, or we shouldn't believe that sneaky suspicion we have about them, that we can't trust our own instincts - doesn't make them better people. It simply makes them more resourceful concealers, and it makes those of us who buy into it stupid consumers.

I urge you, as you read this novel, to not be a stupid consumer - to trust your instincts. As you read these stories you will believe you know who I am talking about and you may be right. Trust your gut. I urge you to see these celebrities for who they are, which is probably not so different from you and me.

With that being said, let me be clear and state what needs to be stated, because I do not want to be sued. This novel is fiction. As such, I have to put in the customary line stating that "All characters appearing in this work are fictitious. Any resemblance to real persons, living or dead, is purely coincidental."

However, I am telling you, the consumer, to read between the lines. Look at the clues.

Can we be honest for a moment? In some of these cases, we all knew that something was off. We wondered if a certain celebrity had really been pregnant, if they really carried their own baby, or if the baby was theirs. We speculated, argued, debated, but we weren't quite sure. Celebrities count on our ignorance. To them we are stupid consumers, who do, say, and believe everything they tell us to do, say, and believe. They count on our ignorance, our stupidity. And moreover, our ignorance and our stupidity make them rich.

As consumers, I believe we are smarter than they think. As you read this novel use your common sense. If it looks like a duck and quacks like a duck - even if they tell us it's a guerrilla - we know that it is a duck. I hope that you enjoy this "novel", and that it answers the questions you always knew you had.

Enjoy!

Prologue

I don't know why I am finally speaking out about this, especially since having babies for celebrities has made me so much money. I think the reason is the last couple I worked for. Something about them really got under my skin. Perhaps it was their arrogance. I mean, who shuts down the hospital floor for their baby so that even the other mothers who are having babies are denied access? And who leaves the hospital in armored vehicles, I mean, what is it that they just had, the Dalai Lama?

But, truthfully, maybe it wasn't their arrogance. After all, I've had babies for many arrogant celebrities. I think what angered me so much was how they disregarded me. It's not that I want any special praise. I mean, after all, it's a job for me and nothing else. I don't become attached to the babies. But I do want to be treated with some modicum of respect. Is that too much to ask?

This couple disrespected me and treated me like I was some groupie. After I had their precious baby (by C-section because she did not want "their" baby to pass through my vagina), they moved me to a nondescript hospital room to heal. They did not allow me to have any visitors, and the one nurse that was allowed to care for me was their personal nurse, and she was mean as hell.

After two days of living in this white room, with no windows, and no visitors, I was handed a cool five million dollars and escorted from the hospital in the middle of the night by a security guard. I was told never to discuss this, never to tell anyone, never to mention them, and never to even come to any of their concerts. The only thing they didn't tell me was to drop dead, which I know they wished I would so that all evidence of what had happened could disappear. I wanted them to at least acknowledge me. I imagine they treat their gardeners better than they did me.

Well, guess what? I've had it. Theirs was the last baby that I will carry; I am done with this job. But not before I tell it all. Not before I tell every dirty secret.

Chapter 1: Detour

Contrary to what you might be thinking, I started out with a normal childhood. I was not molested, raped, abandoned, or any of the other drama that might result in choosing a different type of lifestyle like the one I chose. I was raised by my mom and dad, both of whom were school teachers and loved me very much. I had no brothers or sisters, nor did I want any. I totally enjoyed having my mom and dad all to myself. I was a straight A student and an athlete, having ran track for much of my elementary and high school years.

Admittedly I am not very beautiful. I am actually rather plain-looking. Plain hair, plain skin, plain features, average height. This used to drive me crazy growing up, and I always wished I was prettier, more stand-out looking. I always just seemed to fade into the background.

I couldn't have known at the time that my plainness and my ability to fade into the background would serve me well in my future profession as a celebrity surrogate. After all, nobody wants the surrogate to draw attention to herself, or have some weird or special feature or characteristic that might be passed on to the celebrity's child.

The celebrities always wanted me to be as inconsequential as possible, and lucky for them all my life I have been.

In high school I didn't have any boyfriends and managed to stay a virgin until college. Because I was so smart, I won a full scholarship to a university, which made mom and dad really proud. Mom and dad waited until after my high school graduation to present me with a used Honda Civic they'd bought for me because I'd won a full scholarship and they wouldn't have to pay any tuition.

When I got to college, instead of "wilding out" like a lot of college freshmen do, I decided to focus on my studies so that I could graduate in three years instead of four. I majored in prelaw, with plans to become a lawyer, and make mom and dad proud. I took 21 hours of credits every semester, and in the summers I took 12 hours which was considered full time. I was on the President's list, the Dean's list, and tutored after classes to earn myself some extra money.

I mostly saved all my money so that I could help fund my law school tuition. My one indulgence was celebrity gossip magazines. I absolutely loved them, and I followed the lives of stars the way some people follow the bible. I wanted to know who was wearing what, who was dating whom, what star was having a baby, who was cheating, where they went out to dinner, etcetera.

I'd finish my class assignments, early of course, and then I'd sit back in the bathtub in my shared dorm room and read my celebrity gossip magazines from front to back, even taking notes with a yellow highlighter. I would highlight my favorite celebrity's favorite shoes, and the newest shade of nail polish all the stars were wearing.

I fantasized that I would become an attorney for the stars, litigating endorsement deals for them and living among them with my nice house and nice cars and money galore. I imagined that they would know my name and I'd have their phone numbers on speed dial. They would need me to negotiate their successful contracts and I would finally become consequential.

I carried this fantasy with me for two and a half years. Every time a class got harder, I imagined the stars I would meet, the life I would live, if I just kept my head on straight and worked hard in school.

One year before I was due to graduate, I finally met a boy. His name was Eddie and he was a tutor like me. Our initial conversations were about effective tutoring strategies and study plans for the students we tutored. As time went on, we met for coffee a few times but always to discuss something about tutoring. I wasn't particularly attracted to Eddie, but he was a really nice guy and I did enjoy hanging out with him.

Eventually we became friends and, realizing that I was tired of being a virgin, I decided that I would give my virginity to Eddie. I didn't want to go to law school a virgin. I wanted to be taken seriously. I wanted to be seen as a woman. I figured losing my virginity would give me an air of sophistication, experience and maturity, so I decided Eddie would help me lose my virginity and become a woman.

We were at his little studio apartment, and had just finished watching a popular television show, when I reached over and kissed him. He pulled back from the kiss and looked at me real funny-like. Not to be detoured, and because I had set my mind to losing my virginity, I kissed him again and this time he did not pull back. He kissed me back, and the next thing I knew he was laying on top of me, both of us fully clothed.

He rolled off of me and pulled off his shirt. Assuming it was my turn to go next, I pulled off my shirt too. He then pulled off his pants. I did the same. He left his boxers on and lay on top of me on the sofa. I had on my underwear too. He pulled his penis out through the slit in his boxers and attempted to put it inside of me. I opened my legs wider to allow him access, but I was scared. I wondered how badly this would hurt and if I should ask about a condom. I didn't want to ask him if this would hurt, and I didn't want to ask about a condom because I didn't want to come off as inexperienced.

Little did I know, this was Eddie's first time too. He slid his penis inside of me, and it did hurt. Over and over he kept trying to push it in deeper and deeper inside of me but it wouldn't go. All the attempts were hurting me more and more and I was about to change my mind and tell Eddie that we needed to stop.

As if reading my mind, Eddie jumped up and grabbed some Vaseline. He rubbed it on the tip of his penis and tried again. This time Eddie's penis went inside of me and Eddie nearly lost his mind. He started cursing and stuttering and he rammed his penis harder and harder into my vagina, all the while muttering something about how tight it was.

After about 45 seconds he came inside of me and we just lay there. He was panting as if he'd run a marathon and I was laying there wondering what would happen next. Within a couple minutes Eddie fell asleep, and I lay there wondering how I would get him off me.

Eventually I maneuvered my body enough to where he slid off of me, and there we lay side by side. He was still asleep, snoring like a bear, as I hurried to get dressed. After I finished dressing and cleaning myself off, I left. The next day as we were tutoring, Eddie barely looked at me. He seemed so into the tutoring that I thought nothing of it. I figured it must've been a challenging student.

After our shifts were over, I asked him if he wanted to grab a bite to eat and he made up some excuse about having to be somewhere. As the days went by, he avoided me more and more, until eventually he stopped speaking to me entirely. Although I wondered what I did wrong, I didn't have much time to process it all, because at the end of that month my period didn't come. I did not think I could get pregnant my first time, but I still went to the local health clinic to determine if I was pregnant.

After a three hour wait, and a five minute pregnancy test, I discovered that I was indeed pregnant. I was stunned that after a 45 second sexual encounter – if you could even call it an encounter - I would now be responsible for another life as a single mom. Although I didn't necessarily believe in abortion, I knew it was my only option. My being pregnant, in college, single and unwed, would have killed my parents, and who knows what it would have done to my dreams of becoming a lawyer for celebrities.

For the next several weeks I saved up all my tutoring money – because I didn't want to taint my law school savings - and finally when I was only $100 short I called my parents and asked them if I could have $100 to take a paralegal course. I told them that if I was a paralegal, I could make some good money and earn some experience on my way to becoming a lawyer. Although money was always tight for them, my parents sent the money the next day. They were always in support of all things academic. I hated lying to them.

When the money came the next day, I just cried. For the first time I was disgusted with myself. I drove myself to have the abortion and waited the appropriate amount of time after it was over so that I could drive myself home. I never even told Eddie what had happened. Although I continued to see him around campus from time to time, he barely even spoke to me.

After the abortion, something died inside of me. Although I was in my second to last semester, I began to slack off and my grades dropped. Initially, my professors let me slide. They knew I had been a hardworking student, and although they didn't know what had changed in me, they thought I'd snap out of it and get back into the swing of things. By midterms I was near failing and my professors could no longer ignore what was happening with me. They set up meetings with me, and warned me that I was dangerously close to ruining my GPA and possibly losing my scholarship. By then I was afraid. Not for myself, but I was scared of disappointing my parents.

I finally turned to mom and dad, and although I didn't tell them that I'd had an abortion, I did tell them that I was having a hard time and needed some help. Mom and dad called me every day on the phone and really began to lift me out of the dark place I had slipped into. Thanksgiving break was coming up, and although I desperately missed my family and wanted to see them, I had decided to stay on campus to try to catch up on my schoolwork and salvage my GPA and my scholarship. My parents, being as awesome as they are, decided they'd come to me instead.

My parents were scheduled to drive down to my campus two days before Thanksgiving. In the meantime I locked myself in my dorm room, wrote extra papers, and completed my regular assignments as well as any extra credit work that I could get. By the time that Tuesday came around, I was feeling hopeful that I would emerge from this semester back on track. The icing on the cake occurred when I received an acceptance letter into a great law school for after graduation. Although it wasn't my law school of choice, it was a great school and I was becoming excited again and getting back to my old self.

That Tuesday before Thanksgiving, I talked to mom and dad before they left the house, since neither of them had a cell phone. They informed me that they'd be there by 6 p.m., and would take me to a nice dinner. It was 10 a.m., and I knew they had an eight hour drive ahead of them, so I wished them a safe trip, and decided to tidy up before they got there.

After I got my side of the dorm room spic and span (my roommate had gone home for the holidays), I decided to settle down with a celebrity gossip magazine. This would be the first time I'd have read a celebrity gossip magazine since all this happened. I ran to the local drugstore and picked up the magazine, as well as my mom's and my favorite ice cream. I then settled in for a good read. It was about 5 p.m. by then and I read and waited, hoping the remaining hour would pass quickly.

At around 7 p.m. my parents still had not gotten there, but I wasn't worried because I knew that my dad didn't believe in driving even one mile over the speed limit, so it wasn't unusual for them to be late. At some point I must have dozed off, because when I woke it was 10 p.m. and there was still no word from my parents.

I must admit I was beginning to get a bit worried by then. I didn't feel like anything bad had happened, because I knew that I would've felt something if something bad had happened to them, but I was worried that maybe they were broken down on the side of the road or out of gas. I assured myself that my daddy would have had the car fully serviced before even going for a thirty minute drive, let alone eight hours, and that he would've never let the car run out of gas. So why were they late?

I began to pace the floor, not sure what else to do. Mom and dad had no brothers or sisters, both were only children like me, so there was no one else I could call to check on them. Finally at about midnight I said a prayer and began to call the local hospitals. There were no reports of any accidents, so I just waited. I felt so alone. I was tempted to call Eddie, but by then we were no longer friends. So I just waited and waited.

Sometime around 4 a.m. there was a knock on my door. I bolted out of my chair, where I'd been sitting for the last several hours drinking cups of coffee to stay awake and wait for my parents, and ran to the door. I expected to see my parents, looking rather sheepish about worrying me. It had occurred to me that my parents might have slipped off to some place, or to indulge in an activity while on their way to see me. I reasoned that maybe they had stopped somewhere to have a little time to themselves.

My parents loved each other so much, and I know they worked so hard, and rarely took a vacation, so I thought maybe they scheduled in a little vacation time together. That thought had eased my mind, and allowed me to worry a bit less.

When I got to the door, ready to good-naturedly fuss at them for running off like teenagers and worrying me half to death, I was surprised to see the sheriff and two officers at my door.

A reason didn't automatically occur to me for why the sheriff and the officers would be on my doorstep. I even remember looking past them to see if my parents would be arriving behind them. I was afraid my parents would pull up right when the sheriff and officers were on my doorstep and think that something had happened to me.

I half-heartedly heard the sheriff say something about a car accident, and being sorry, or something like that. My knees began to tremble even though I didn't fully comprehend what they were saying to me. Apparently something inside of me did comprehend what was going on because as soon as they muttered the words "Your parents are dead" I distinctly remember one of the officers reaching out to catch me as I hit the floor. I had fainted.

When I awoke I was in the back of the patrol car with one of the officers driving. We arrived at a town about two hours away from where I was attending college. Apparently my mom and dad had been in a car accident with an 18-wheeler that had veered off the road when the driver fell asleep. My dad was killed instantly. My mom survived for one hour and died while in surgery.

It had taken this long to find me because my parents did not have a cell phone and my mom's purse had been thrown from the car and was not located for a long time.

When the officers realized that my parents had a college-aged daughter in the next town over, instead of calling me to come to the hospital, they thought they'd come to me personally. They were nice enough to want to ease the burden of having me drive there to hear the news.

I listened to all this in and out of consciousness. When I did wake, I alternated between asking where my parents were and mumbling about not wanting to live. As a result of my ramblings, the doctors put me on some psychotropic drugs and made me sleep.

I awoke to learn that I had been placed on suicide watch. And they were right to do that because the first chance I got I was going to end things on this earth. Though I had been raised a Christian and didn't believe in suicide, I knew I could not go on living without my parents. Here I was 20 years old and all alone. No family, no one.

Three days later, when I was "better," I was approached about making funeral arrangements and had to be medically tranquilized again from the sheer stress of it all. Two days after that I was released in time to attend my parents' funeral. Because I could not stomach making the arrangements, someone at the hospital had done it for me. Apparently there are people who do that.

When I got to the funeral home and looked at the caskets, I remember thinking that the caskets suited my parents. They were simple, yet elegant. They were very understated, but beautiful. My parents had been the same way. They were modest, frugal, thoughtful, simple people. They loved me, they loved each other, and they loved being educators.

Several of their current and former students attended the funeral, but I did not see or say much. I passed thru the funeral in a trance. It seemed like my mind and body was keeping me purposefully foggy so as to lessen the severity of what was happening.

When everything was over, at the end of the day, I was all alone in my parents' house. I walked around their house, remembering the table where I had bumped my mouth as a child and lost my first tooth. The vanity where my mom applied her mascara, the only makeup she ever wore. The black house-slippers that I gave my dad for father's day many years ago. They were faded and worn, but dad had refused to replace them because they had come from me.

After a few minutes it all became too much. I grabbed a duffle bag, picked out a few things to bring with me from the home, like a picture of mom and dad, a picture of the 3 of us, mom's cookbook with all her favorite recipes, and dad's day planner with all his little inspirational scribbles in the margins. I cleaned out the refrigerator to prevent the items from spoiling, and locked the house, never to return again. At the age of twenty, just two months shy of my twenty-first birthday, I was all alone in the world. This would be the beginning of the end for me.

Chapter 2: Searching for Something

Although I know it pained mom and dad from heaven, especially since I only had one semester left, I dropped out of college. The truth is, I just didn't care anymore. Not about school, or about life. Having dropped out of school I no longer had the dorm room to live in and I was not going to stay at mom and dad's because it hurt too much. So, courtesy of an advance from my parents' attorney, I was staying at an extended stay hotel.

Over the course of the two months since my parents had died, I had put on over twenty pounds from having takeout fast-food delivered to me every day and sleeping the days away. I didn't get any hair trims, so my hair was growing really long, which surprisingly enough made me look more attractive. I barely took baths and spent my twenty-first birthday watching old marathons of America's Next Top Model.

The day after I turned 21, I had an appointment with my parents' attorney to discuss my parents' will. I had not known that they'd even had a will. I at least took a shower before leaving my "new home," and even that was an effort. When I arrived at the attorneys' office, she just gasped when she saw me. I knew I looked bad, but I really didn't care. I listened half-heartedly while she explained all the deductions she'd made from my parents' "estate." As I daydreamed about the last family trip my parents and I had taken, I heard her say something about paying off their house, paying for their funeral expenses, repaying the advance I'd been given to have someplace to stay, and deducting her fee. She then handed me a check across the table.

I remember being surprised that there was money left over after all of that. I remember thinking that I hope there's enough left for a deposit on an apartment, and that I'd have to quickly get a job to cover rent on an apartment. Or I'd live out of my car if there wasn't enough for a deposit on an apartment. I didn't care. I turned the check over right about the time the attorney was saying something about me being responsible with my newfound wealth. Something about my being a millionaire at the age of 21, and getting help making smart financial decisions.

I looked at the check, half expecting that I'd heard her wrong, especially since I hadn't been listening in the first place. The check read $2,101,609.27. I had a check for over two million dollars in my hand. Surprisingly, my first thought was to tear it up. I felt like God was trying to pay me off for taking my mom and dad, and I wanted him to know that two million would not be enough. No amount was. But what I did instead surprised both myself and my parents' attorney.

I laughed. I laughed and laughed until I couldn't catch my breath. I laughed so long and hard that I peed my pants. The attorney just looked at me with such a sad expression. I know she thought I was losing it, or had already. But even her expression was funny. So that made me laugh harder.

Even though the attorney thought I was delirious, the real reason I was laughing was at my parents. This check, to me, was classic mom and dad. My dad had a saying "The bigger the house, the smaller the bank account." Although I'd chalked that up to the rants of a frugal old man, especially as a teenager when all I had wanted was to have a bigger house, a nicer car for my parents, and name brand clothes for myself.

I'd never put much stock into what my dad said. My parents had lived that saying, however, choosing to live modestly so that they could retire comfortably and leave a sizable nest egg for me. My parents had saved and invested enough to be able to retire on one million dollars, and still leave one million dollars for me. Their big surprise was that they were also going to pay for my law schooling, with one check right up front.

I explained the reason I was laughing to my parents' attorney, and she smiled sadly, remembering how my parents had approached her about their plan to send me to law school debt free, and with an upgraded car. My dad had his eyes on a Toyota Avalon for me, which knowing my dad was the epitome of luxury.

I said my goodbyes to the attorney, promised to follow-up with the financial planner she'd found for me, and left her office.

The first place I went was to church. Usually the church is locked, but for some reason that day it wasn't. I sat in the back of the pew and talked to God and my parents. I wanted to know what they wanted me to do with the money. I wondered should I donate the whole thing to the church? Go back to school and become an attorney like I'd planned and make my parents proud? Deep down in my heart I knew I did not want to become an attorney. I knew that was something I was doing for my parents. My heart was no longer on school. I struggled with what to do.

Ultimately what made up my mind were my parents themselves. Here, they'd saved and invested diligently for a retirement that would never come. They had made sacrifices for nothing. Every delayed vacation, and every delayed indulgence ended the night my parents were killed. In my mind my parents had lived for tomorrow and it had not come. I did not want that. All my life I had been diligent, and studious, a downright nerd. I had never just lived for the day, let alone in the moment. I decided right then that I would do what they had not been given the chance to do. I decided that I would live life to the fullest, and that I would do it for me and for them.

I went back to the extended stay hotel and looked around at my belongings. All I had brought with me were several pairs of sweatpants - which at this point was all I could fit - some oversized shirts that I'd recently bought from Wal-Mart to accommodate my recently expanding girth, a few toiletries, and the items I'd picked up from my parent' house. I decided to leave it all there, except for what I'd taken from mom and dad's and the clothes on my back. And of course my toothbrush. I settled up at the front desk, paid my bill, and was on my way to bigger and better things.

The first night out of the extended stay hotel I went to the most expensive hotel in town, which just so happened to be a Hilton. I checked in with money left over from my advance, ordered room service, and took the best bath of my life. The bed was so comfortable and I'd never felt anything so luxurious before. Lord knows it was a far cry from my dorm room bed. Although I cried myself to sleep that night like I did every night since mom and dad's death, at least that night I did it on a feather-soft bed surrounded by what I considered at the time to be luxury. The next day I left the room to go cash my new check.

On the way to the bank, I stopped in at an expensive department store and bought a cute pantsuit. I wanted to look good when I cashed my check. After leaving the bank, with varying looks of admiration, shock from the bank manager, and a little bit of envy, I went back to the Hilton and ordered room service again. While taking what was becoming my nightly bath, I grabbed a notepad to chart my course. I needed to figure out what I was going to do and where I was going to go. Since money wouldn't be a problem, I knew I could go anywhere. As someone who'd never gone anywhere before, except for the occasional family trip to the beach, I didn't have the first idea where to go.

After sitting in the tub for over an hour, I had only managed to jot down "Disney World" and "Hawaii." I ruled both of those out when I rationalized that Disney World seemed to be for children and Hawaii seemed like it was for couples. So where did a single adult go to have some fun? After getting out of the bathtub I must have drifted off to sleep because when I awoke my television was on TMZ and they were in Las Vegas covering a story about a few socialites and celebrities that were in the city. I thought that was a sign that that's where I should be, so I pulled out my newly acquired laptop and booked a first class flight to Las Vegas.

Although I don't like to use profanity, the only words I can use to describe first class are "The Shit!" The seats were so roomy, the service impeccable, and the drinks tasty. In first class, during that flight, was the first time I had ever had champagne, and I decided that I would become a connoisseur with my newfound wealth.

When I got to Las Vegas, I immediately checked into the hotel that I had seen on TMZ last night. Because it was so expensive to be there, and because I did not know how long I was going to be there, I stayed in a standard room, no suites for me this time.

I began my trip with a shopping spree. In college I had always wore jeans and cute little tops, but I decided to change my look to accommodate my new status as a millionaire. I went shopping and bought pants, suits, silk blouses, and cocktail dresses. I also bought enough pairs of shoes to furnish an entire small city. No more flip flops for me.

My first week in Las Vegas I spent shopping during the daytime and ordering room service and movies from pay-per-view at night. I also ordered lots of champagne. I realized I had a great affinity for the stuff. The first few times I ordered it I caught a buzz and jumped up and down on the bed and danced myself into a frenzy in the comfort of my own hotel room, but after a few more tries I realized I was a natural and started to venture out into newer, bolder drinks.

Pretty soon I grew bored with sitting in my hotel room all night long. At some point I had stopped putting myself to sleep crying for mom and dad. I had even started having a few thoughts about Eddie. I wondered what he was doing. One evening after I picked up the phone and dialed his number, then hung up, I realized that it wasn't Eddie that I was missing. It was companionship. At that point I decided to venture out into the hotel casinos with the hopes of meeting someone. Not a guy necessarily, but maybe a friend.

Instead of meeting potential friends, however, I met total creeps. I was approached by men who thought I was a lonely woman who they could hook up with, and although I was lonely, I wasn't that desperate. I met women who either propositioned me for sex, or offered me jobs in the sex industry. Although I was flattered that they thought I could work in the sex industry, I was also scared out of my mind. I was so scared, in fact, that I stopped hanging out in casinos and started to go to nightclubs.

The first club I went to was supposed to be a "hotspot" according to Google reviews, but it was actually a hole in the wall that smelled like Chinese food. The second club I went to was a little better, but the crowd was really young and the music was too loud, plus I was way overdressed. I had worn a cute little black dress with some really cute needlepoint stilettos, but most of the girls were in denim skirts or summer dresses, with platform heels. Needless to say, I felt totally out of place. I decided that I needed some help picking a proper club, so I asked the front desk clerk at the hotel where I was staying for some recommendations. I had noticed her many times during my stay at the hotel and she always seemed so nicely dressed and stylish. There was a certain flair to her.

One evening I struck up a conversation with her and she pointed me in the direction of what she called a "great" club. I went and although I spent the whole night sitting at the bar drinking champagne, it was still a great club and I felt that it was right up my alley. The music was jumping, though not so loud that it felt as if it was pounding in my chest. The floors were shiny and clean, the people were dressed stylishly without looking like they had put too much effort into it, and the vibe was just right. With nothing else to do, I started going there every night of the week.

A few nights later, I saw the front desk clerk from the hotel there. She came up and talked to me and asked how I liked the place. I told her that it was just my style, and she invited me to her table to hang out with her friends. When I got to the table, I was taken aback by how beautiful these girls all were. They were breathtaking. The front desk girl introduced everyone, including herself. Her name was Sammi, and her friends were Rachel, Lisa, and Racquel. They were all in the service industry, as either front desk clerks, retail store clerks, or waitresses, and they were all so glamorous-looking.

Although my clothes were as nice as theirs, maybe even nicer, certainly more expensive, they all seemed to have a sophistication that I did not. And where I considered myself pretty plain-looking, they were all exotically beautiful. And as if to prove my point, men (and even some women) sent them drinks all night long.

They spent the night alternating between declining some drinks, accepting others, and dancing the night away. Whereas I was always in my own head - thinking, analyzing, wondering and questioning - they seemed so carefree. They danced and laughed and flirted the night away. And I spent the night thinking that I should also be dancing and enjoying myself, instead of analyzing what they were wearing, wondering what made them so beautiful and questioning why I wasn't carefree. I thought that I should've been having more fun, maybe even the most fun, especially since I was the wealthiest person at the table. At the end of the night, I was exhausted and I hadn't even danced. I had worn myself out just from thinking so much.

I saw Sammi many more times after that and she even invited me to more clubs and outings with her and her friends. After about a month, she and I became fast friends. Being around her increased my confidence and I began to say more, do more, and "let down my hair more."

When we went out I danced without wondering who was looking. I accepted drinks from guys and had even gone on a couple dates, though it was never anything serious. I had already bought beautiful clothes, but now I had the confidence to wear the clothes the right way, without feeling like I was playing dress up in my mom's closet.

Pretty soon Sammi and I decided to get an apartment together. I had told Sammi that my parents died in a car crash and had left me some money. When we went apartment looking, Sammi wanted to find an apartment that was within a certain price range, but because Sammi had been such a good friend to me and had changed my life, I told her I would pay for the apartment, and all she had to do was buy the groceries. Sammi and I found a great luxury apartment in the heart of Las Vegas. It was a three-bedroom apartment with a doorman in the lobby, an indoor heated pool in the complex, and a spa on the premises.

Sammi and I did everything together when she wasn't at work. She was the sister and the friend that I had never had. So since her birthday was coming up, I decided to surprise her with a first class trip to New York to see her favorite artist. She'd had a crush on this artist since she was a teenager and although he was married, all she wanted was to sleep with him. She believed without a doubt that he was her soul mate, and since this person was always in the news with "speculation of marriage problems" and there were always rumors of infidelity and divorce, she figured she would have a chance with him. She always said that if she could just get him to see her, he would fall in love. So I thought it was a no-brainer that I get us backstage passes to his concert.

On Sammi's birthday we all went out to eat and after we'd had drinks (I had become quite the drinker by then) and dinner, I presented her with the first class tickets to New York, the reservation to stay at a luxurious hotel, and as the finale, the backstage passes to her favorite artists' concert.

Sammi was overjoyed and literally screamed in the restaurant, catching the attention of all who were in attendance. She wrapped her arms around me and said that she loved me, and that I was the sister she'd always wanted (even though Sammi had a sister they were never close). I was flattered and as she and I hugged and cried together, I realized that this was the first time in a long time that I had felt loved.

Chapter 3: Game Changer

We arrived in New York, first class, and checked into our hotel. We then went shopping for something new to wear to the concert. Even though Sammi knew I was rich she never tried to get money from me, and often argued with me when I tried to pay for things. She insisted that she would pay for her own outfit for the concert. She said that I had paid for enough.

I have to admit that Sammi had a way of putting together the cutest outfits for next to nothing. Truth be told, Sammi was so beautiful that she could wear a sackcloth and still look stylish. We picked out our outfits — I went to the high-end boutiques and she went to a department store. We then spent the next couple days drinking, partying, and living it up as we waited for the concert.

On the day of the concert, Sammi and I had spa treatments; everything from manicures and pedicures to facials and deep-tissue massages. We then went to a fancy dinner, and back to the hotel to get dressed.

Sammi wore this really simple but chic navy blue A-line minidress with navy blue pumps and I must admit that she looked flawless as always. I wore this sequined minidress with silver strappy stilettos and I must have looked amazing because when I emerged from my side of the suite Sammi was speechless. When she regained her composure she went on to exclaim how beautiful I was and joked that she should have worn my dress tonight since she was meeting her future husband or baby-daddy. We laughed and agreed that I would let her borrow the dress one day, and off we went to the concert.

When we got to the limo that I had reserved and were escorted into the backseat by the handsome limo driver, he could not take his eyes off me and proceeded to flirt shamelessly. I was honored and soaked up the attention. We drank like fish while on the way to the concert. By the time we got to the venue, I was slightly tipsy and was ready to have some fun.

For the first time Sammi appeared nervous and barely spoke as we were escorted to the backstage area to meet her favorite artist. Sammi stepped into the restroom to freshen up, and I walked around the refreshment tables nibbling on party mix, in an attempt to put something more in my stomach and slow down the effects of the alcohol.

As I was walking around the table nibbling, a guy came over and started talking to me. I couldn't tell if the guy was handsome or not because he had on dark black shades and a ballcap pulled low over his eyes. It didn't matter to me if the guy was good-looking or not, because guys had been flirting with me all night, so I was already in flirt mode.

The guy and I talked and laughed, and pretty soon I was genuinely enjoying myself. This guy had a great sense of humor and I couldn't stop laughing.

Sammi was still not back from the restroom and over 30 minutes had passed, so I went to check on her. When I got into the restroom I saw that Sammi had become sick, probably from a combination of the alcohol and nerves, and had been throwing up in the commode. Her usually flawless skin was now streaked with running mascara, and her usually flawless hair was now wildly strewn about.

I grabbed my clutch and pulled out my makeup – and a breath mint – and fixed Sammi back up. She asked me if her guy had come out yet and I told her that he had not, but that I had met a great guy with a great sense of humor.

Eager to see my new guy, whom I had nicknamed "Shades" (because of the dark black shades he was wearing), and to see if her favorite artist had shown up yet, Sammi and I emerged from the bathroom.

I walked over to my guy smiling from ear to ear and after I got to him, and received the little squeeze that he gave me (which made me feel all tingly inside) I noticed that Sammi was not next to me. When I turned around I saw that Sammi was still standing at the door of the restroom with her mouth wide open.

I went to her to see what was wrong, figuring she was about to get sick again, and heard Sammi whisper, "That's him!" I said "Who's who?" while looking in the direction that she was pointing and she said, "Him! That's him!" Again I said "Who's him?" and Sammi said "My guy's your guy!" I turned around so slowly that somebody would've thought that I was in The Matrix. I had unknowingly met Sammi's guy but didn't know it since he was in disguise at his own backstage event!

When I saw what I thought was my guy smiling at me, and I saw my best friend looking heartbroken, I immediately went into "fix it" mode. I had only met this guy 30 minutes prior, so I wasn't attached.

I grabbed Sammi by the hand and walked her over to her favorite artist/future husband (once he divorced his current wife). I made the introductions and told Sammi's guy how big a fan she was and that all she wanted was to meet him. All the while we talked, however, he only spoke to me. So I excused myself from the conversation and walked back over to the snack table, in an attempt to give my girl some alone time with her guy.

When I glanced up they were talking and I felt good, albeit a little sad. I got over it real quick though because this guy was Sammi's guy and had I known he was who he was (if he hadn't had on those dark shades and that ballcap), I would never have talked to him.

About 15 minutes later Sammi came over and still smiling, though seemingly a bit heartbroken, informed me that her guy kept asking about me. The whole time they were talking they had been talking about me! Sammi, seeing how into this guy I had been (before I knew he was hers) and how into me he seemed, gave him our number so that he could call me.

I loved Sammi too much and vowed never to talk to this guy if he ever called. I doubted he would call, being as famous as he was and with so many women to choose from. But if he did call I decided I wouldn't speak to him. Although Sammi seemed cool, and even joked about not standing in the way of fate, I didn't want to take the chance of this guy coming between us and losing my best friend. And I also wasn't into the married man's spiel about "getting a divorce" or "we're not really together." Being in Las Vegas, I had met many men with the same story and I just wasn't biting. Sammi and I went on to enjoy the rest of the concert and I put the thought of "Shades" out of my mind.

A couple weeks later, we were back in Las Vegas and it was business as usual. I had long ago decided I would become a club promoter. Being in Las Vegas, and given the fact that I had made going out to new clubs my "job", it seemed like the perfect business to get into. Sammi was still working at the hotel but had applied to become their Events Coordinator and gotten the job.

Given her outgoing personality, I wasn't surprised she had landed the job. I was really excited that Sammi and I had similar goals in mind, so she and I made plans to go into business together once I figured out how to become a club promoter and after she had made some contacts and connections being the Events Coordinator for such a major, high-end, party-type hotel.

One day after I got back to our place, after having lunch with a seasoned promoter who had decided to take me under his wing and show me the club promotion business, I got a call from "Shades". If felt weird to talk to him, even though I had gotten Sammi's blessing, so I kept the conversation short – almost to the point of being rude. The next day he sent me flowers, and the day after that he sent more. He did that for a week straight until even Sammi was like "Girl, talk to the man!"

The following day when he sent yet another dozen roses, I called him. He didn't sound surprised to hear from me, which kind of annoyed me.

The first question out of my mouth was about his marriage. He told me that his wife had been his high school sweetheart and had been with him even before he became rich and famous. He said that they did not have a marriage, but had agreed to "stay together" throughout her sickness.

He confided that his wife had ovarian cancer and was undergoing chemotherapy, so they had agreed to delay the divorce until she was through with treatment. He told me that he was not physically attracted to his wife and that they had not been intimate in at least two years – one year before her diagnosis and this current year as she had been going through her cancer treatment. He told me that he loved her and always would, but that they had both grown apart.

I wanted so badly to not believe him, but he sounded so sincere. I mean, he told me everything about anything I asked about. Like the fact that he'd had affairs throughout their marriage and his wife knew and didn't care as long as he did his "dirt" discreetly.

I told him I was not interested in being his "dirt" and he laughed. He didn't try to delude me with talks of marriage. He just wanted to get to know me and hopefully become good enough friends so that he could come and visit me when he was in town. I told him not to get ahead of himself and he just laughed.

What's funny is how fast "Shades" and I got close. Over the next several months we became such good friends that he had been by to visit on a number of occasions, and even he and Sammi were cool. Meanwhile, Sammi had moved on and met a guy at an events conference and they were getting pretty serious.

"Shades" came to see me on my birthday and he gave me a paid trip to an island in Mexico, with two first class tickets. Although he probably thought I would take Sammi, I decided to take him with me, and he was delighted.

While in Mexico, "Shades" and I could not go out publicly together because he didn't want the media to see us since they didn't know the "arrangement" between him and his wife. He said he didn't want to complicate the issue and feed the media's fire. So during the days I shopped and shopped some more, and during the nights "Shades" and I became intimate for the first time.

The sex was good, but I think it was made better by the fact that I was falling in love with "Shades", and in spite of myself was beginning to imagine a future with him. I wanted so badly to tell him, but I didn't want to ruin what we had. I think truthfully I didn't want to scare "Shades" off.

I had met a lot of men while living in Las Vegas as a single, wealthy, attractive woman, but I had yet to feel this way about anyone. "Shades" and I went on like this for several more months, and one year from the day we met we made plans to have an anniversary dinner in a nice restaurant.

"Shades'" wife was getting better. She was off chemotherapy and regaining weight, so "Shades" started telling me that he would be able to be out in public with me soon. I was so excited and truly felt like it would be our coming out, especially since I hadn't heard any more stories about "Shades" cheating on his wife, or being caught with any other women. That led me to believe that he was being faithful to me and that he felt as strongly about me as I did about him.

A week before our scheduled one year anniversary date, "Shades" called me up and told me he had something important to tell me. He sounded funny on the phone, almost nervous, and I knew in that instant that he was going to propose. I confided in Sammi my suspicions that "Shades" was going to propose and she was so happy for me.

A couple days before our scheduled date, when "Shades" was due to arrive in town, I came down with the flu. I guess the excitement of it all must have gotten to me. I had no energy and no appetite and just slept and slept. Sammi told me that I should go see someone, and took the day off to go with me to the doctor. When we got there, the doctor examined me, and confirmed my suspicions, that I did in fact have the flu but also that I was seven weeks pregnant. I nearly fell off the table. I explained to him that I couldn't possibly be pregnant. That I'd never missed a single pill since I started birth control after an incident in college (that incident being an unplanned pregnancy). I frantically told him that I couldn't be pregnant because I had taken the pills, religiously, even when I wasn't having sex.

In response, the doctor showed me the ultrasound of the tiny beating "group of cells" and explained to me that the beating was a heartbeat and that the group of cells would one day grow into a little baby. That is, if I chose to continue the pregnancy. I just sat there in stunned silence. I literally couldn't form a thought. I did not feel happy, nor did I feel sad. I literally felt nothing.

While discussing this "miracle birth" the doctor and I uncovered the reason for the unexplained pregnancy. I had been given antibiotics a couple months ago because I'd had strep throat. I didn't know at the time that antibiotics lessened the effectiveness of birth control pills. I didn't have a lot of sexual partners, so I didn't know all the particulars of sex and birth control.

I walked out of the doctor's office in a daze. Oddly enough, although I was stone silent and seemingly cool as a cucumber, Sammi was the emotional one. She was worried for me. My silence scared her.

She took me home and made me some tea, and for the first time I had to ask myself "Is tea something I can have while pregnant?" Without even realizing it, my instinct had been to protect this baby, this life growing inside me. I can't say that I loved the baby, but I knew that I could not and would not proceed with an abortion. The last time I'd done that I had been scarred forever, and I was not willing to do it again.

I was hoping that in time I would grow to love the life inside of me, since it was conceived in love between "Shades" and me. I figured that when he and I saw each other for our upcoming anniversary dinner, and he proposed, I would tell him that I was pregnant. I knew he would be so happy, especially since earlier in our relationship he had confided in me that he always wanted a son, but that his wife had been unable to get pregnant because of all the cysts she had on her ovaries as a young girl, even before they had spotted the cancer. I figured "Shades" would be overjoyed that I was able to give him a baby and that I eventually would grow to feel excited that I was carrying his baby. If nothing else, I was excited about our happily ever after.

Chapter 4: The Beginning of my Life as a Celebrity Surrogate

Eventually I got over the flu and "Shades" and I were able to reschedule our date. Even though he wasn't going to be in town for another several months, he said he didn't want to wait and needed to see me soon. That made me so excited and confirmed my suspicions that he was going to propose.

On the day of our date, I went out and had a spa treatment, a manicure and pedicure. I bought a new dress and new shoes. I also bought "Shades" an expensive watch that I had inscribed with the words "The Beginning." I thought the watch with the inscription "The Beginning" would be a symbol of the beginning of our lifetime together.

At eight o' clock on the dot, the doorman called up to let me know that the limo had arrived. At first I thought it was odd that "Shades" didn't come to get me himself as he had many times before, but then I thought about how sweet it was that he sent a limo. I thought about how he was trying to set a romantic mood, and go all out for our special night. I grabbed my clutch and

"Shades'" watch, which I had neatly and professionally wrapped, and headed out the door.

When I got to "Shades'" hotel, his security let me in then left the room, like they'd done on a few other occasions. I knew he was just giving us the privacy that we'd need for "Shades" to propose.

"Shades" stepped into the room and he wasn't dressed up, but he looked nice. He had on pressed jeans, a white cuffed shirt, and a camel-colored blazer with camel loafers. I thought maybe he was dressed so casually because we were staying in, but it didn't matter.

When I saw him I went to him and wrapped my arms around him so tight. I had missed him, and the fact that I had his baby growing inside me made me feel even closer to him. It made me feel as if he truly belonged to me and that I belonged to him.

"Shades" hugged me briefly then let me go rather abruptly. I could see the nervousness all over his face, and that made me love him more. The whole while we ate, he barely said a word. He was acting so strange, he seemed so nervous, which again made me realize how much I meant to him.

When we were finished with dinner, "Shades" and I went to sit on the sofa, and I told him that I had something for him. He told me he needed to say something first, so I braced myself for his proposal. I was sweating a little bit and thought for the briefest moment that it would have been really cool to be able to call my mom tomorrow to let her know that I was engaged. I was preparing to see "Shades" drop down to one knee and ask me to be his wife. When I heard him say "….wife," although I didn't hear the rest of what he said, I screamed "Yes! Yes!" "Shades" just looked at me confused. We sat like that for a second – me looking at him with so much love and joy, and him looking at me confused - before I elaborated on my acceptance, by saying, "Yes, I will marry you." He blinked his eyes a few times and tilted his head to the side showing his confusion. I remember thinking that the gesture made him look kind of like a dog.

No one spoke a word, and then he repeated what I guess he had said earlier, which was "I'm going back to my wife." In my mind he had said "Will you be my wife" but in reality he had said he was going back to his wife. I instantly felt sick. I literally bent over and puked. "Shades" ran to get a towel, and I just stood there in my own puke. He cleaned up the puke around me and I continued to just stand there. Eventually I managed to ask, then yell, "Well what about babies? You want babies!" And he said, "We [his wife and he] agreed to adopt" and I puked again.

While cleaning up my puke the second time, I heard him explain that while caring for his wife and seeing her fight so hard to live, he began to fall in love with her again. Apparently "Shades" and his wife spending so much time together made them remember how they used to be and it rekindled romantic feelings between them.

"Shades" said that by his wife going through such a harrowing experience, it had awakened something inside her that revived her spirit and made her want to live life to the fullest. He explained to me that he now found her fun again, and passionate and exciting. "Shades" sheepishly told me that they had agreed to give their marriage a second chance and planned to renew their vows in the next six months - which was, oddly enough, the month they were originally married.

"Shades" said his wife knew he had been seeing me, and that he had promised her he would break it off with me. He said he was sorry and didn't want to hurt me because he knew I was catching feelings, but reminded me that he had been honest from the beginning that he did not want anything serious.

When I finally caught my breath, and found my voice, I told him that I was not catching feelings but that I had already caught them and had thought that he was going to propose. He nearly choked on his wine when I said those words and asked me why I thought he was going to propose when he was already married. He said he thought we were just having a good time, and although he was sorry to hurt me that he had been honest. I dropped to the sofa and cried.

I felt so pathetic crying for a man, begging him to be with me, but I loved "Shades" so much, and aside from Sammi, he was all that I had left in the world. And, of course, this child. Our child. I looked up and him with tears streaming down my face and said "But I'm pregnant." He stepped back slowly, and looked down and away from me, seemingly lost in thought. I was hoping to hear him say the words "I made a mistake," "You're the one for me," "The baby must be a sign that we belong together." But what he said instead shocked me. "Shades" said "Give the baby to me."

My mouth dropped open so wide that I almost dislocated my jaw. "Shades" went on to tell me, with a straight face, to give him and his wife the baby, that they were planning to adopt a child anyway, and that they could give the baby a much better life than I could as a single woman who was on the verge of being broke (I had previously confided in "Shades" that I was running out of my inheritance money).

I sat there shocked, and then I got angry. I reached my hand back and slapped "Shades" so hard that I broke two fingernails. I was angry that he broke my heart, and because I felt like he had played with my feelings. I was infuriated that he had the audacity to ask me to give him our baby as if I was giving him a ride to the grocery store.

I grabbed my clutch and the watch that I had bought for him and stormed out of his room. As I walked out the door, I heard him say, "Just think about the baby..."

The next couple weeks found me severely depressed. I didn't eat, couldn't sleep, and despite being pregnant had managed to lose 15 pounds. When Sammi's worry reached a breaking point, she called the doctor and explained to him about my severe depression. Because of my pregnancy, the doctor ordered me into his office.

When I got there, and got examined, the doctor determined that I was severely dehydrated and anemic. He had me admitted to the hospital where I was put on an IV and had to remain there for eight days. During that time, I was put on suicide watch and had to undergo a psychiatric evaluation. During my evaluation the psychiatrist determined that I was suffering from depression and wanted to put me on antidepressants. I declined, because I did not want to harm the baby growing inside me. I did not feel any connection to this child, especially now, but I did not want to harm it nevertheless.

After eight days in the hospital I was released. I know that that hospital stay saved my life. What also saved my life were my daily sessions with the psychiatrist. Talking to her helped me realize that I still had a life to live and that even though "Shades" had broken my heart, I would find love again. But I decided first things first. I would meet "Shades" and his wife, and if she was a good woman, I would let them adopt the baby (I could never bring myself to call it my baby, which I took as a sign that giving the baby up for adoption was meant to be).

It took me a while to get "Shades" on the phone. He was ducking my calls. My guess is that he wanted to make sure I was not going to cause any trouble for him and his wife.

When I finally got him on the phone, he was surprised to hear me say that I forgave him, wished him well with his marriage, and wanted to meet up with him and his wife to determine if they could provide a good home to the baby. He seemed leery of my proposition, like he thought it was a ploy to get him in a room with me. He relaxed after I explained that my intentions were to secure a good home for the baby and that I was going to put the baby up for adoption anyway, that I just preferred it be with people I at least knew. He told me he would talk to his wife and get back to me, but that he was definitely interested.

Two days later he called to tell me he and his wife would love to meet with me. He sent me a first class ticket to his hometown. I did not take Sammi with me because, for one, she didn't believe that I should give the baby up for adoption, especially not to "Shades", and two, I did not want to involve her any further in the messiness that had become my life, especially when I found out that Sammi had become engaged a week ago to that guy she met at the conference but hadn't told me because she hadn't wanted to "throw it in my face" and "make me sad." Well, the same was true for me. I didn't want to make Sammi sad during this time that should've been so joyful for her, so I decided to handle this alone.

The next week, at the agreed upon day and time, I flew out to meet "Shades" and his wife. I had only seen her in the gossip magazines, usually as it pertained to "Shades" cheating on her, so I was not expecting her to meet me personally at the airport. Sure enough though, when I arrived at the baggage check she was there, wearing a cute, short, pixie cut - I guessed because of the chemotherapy - and rocking a fierce pantsuit and stilettos that could've put somebody's eyes out. Although she was probably only about 10 years older than I, I immediately felt like a child in her presence. She exuded confidence and radiance and, funny as it sounds, I was immediately drawn to her.

If I had to describe "Shades'" wife, the word I would use is "cute." She was probably about 5'10, very statuesque, with soft skin and a dimple in her chin. Even though we were in an awkward situation, one that neither of us had ever been in before, she seemed to know what to do. She walked up to me, gave me a big warm hug, and she smelled like luxury. I found myself hugging her back and wanting to be her friend. Although I thought we were going to meet "Shades" right away, she actually took me to lunch first. I think this was her way of letting me get to know her without "Shades" around.

When we got to lunch she ordered and spoke with the waitress as if they were old friends, you'd have never thought she was rich. As fit as she was, I was surprised to see her order a real meal instead of just a salad. I ordered as well and then we started to talk.

"Shades'" wife told me that she knew of me and that she had allowed "Shades" to cheat for many years. She explained to me that the reason she'd done this was because she had believed that stars like "Shades" would cheat anyway, so she had learned to "look the other way." She confided that she was trying to be the type of wife she thought he wanted.

After being diagnosed with cancer, she said that something in her changed. For the first time since she and "Shades" had gotten married, and even while they were dating, she started to think of what she wanted and needed. She realized that she had never lived her life for herself, and that's when she made the decision that she was going to start living life before it was too late.

"Shades'" wife said she went out, she met people, and even began to date. She became happy again, started exercising, and taking better care of herself. This was right around the time that "Shades" started coming around again. She said she could see that he had noticed the change in her and was becoming interested in her again, but she had wanted nothing to do with him. She said he began to court her, and despite herself she began to fall in love with him again.

She actually apologized to me. She said she was sorry if this had caused me any pain. And I believed her. She said it was never her intention to fall back in love with "Shades", but seeing the man that he had become, she was happy that she did. "Shades'" wife said that she was happy to have her husband back and that together they would take great care of his child. She acknowledged that this must be very hard for me and that she appreciated me being woman enough to come and meet with her, even if I chose not to let them adopt the child.

For some reason I found myself getting emotional. Truth be told, I had never felt any real connection with this child. I think the reason I was getting emotional was not because of the child, but because of the sincerity of "Shades'" wife. She spoke with such truth and passion and love that I knew with complete certainty that she would give that same passion and love to the child that I carried.

As we finished lunch and began to leave the restaurant, I told her that she didn't have to take me to meet "Shades", and that I had already made up my mind. I told her that I would be honored if she would adopt this child and love it and take care of it in a way that I wasn't prepared to do. She then got emotional and hugged me so hard that I could barely breathe.

Despite her protests, I had her take me back to the airport. I felt that I had already got all the information I needed. I knew that this child, "Shades" and my child, would be loved unconditionally. I almost felt as if I had gotten pregnant with his child *for her*. It was as if this child was never supposed to be mine, but had always belonged to "Shades" and her. When I got back to Las Vegas, "Shades'" wife had already sent me a bouquet of flowers that said, simply, "Thank You and welcome to our family."

During the first trimester my pregnancy went on without a hitch. "Shades'" wife called me every other day to check on me. When I mentioned my back was already starting to hurt, she had a Shiatsu Antigravity Massage Chair mailed to me. When I mentioned that I had been craving a particular type of food, she had that food delivered to me.

At some point Sammi moved out of our apartment and into a home with her fiancé. I missed Sammi dearly, but I understood that she had to move on with her own life. At first Sammi called me often. We went to lunch, we went to the movies, we even still discussed our plans to open a club promotion business together. But as the months drew on, and as Sammi made plans for her wedding, she and I began to talk less and less. Around the same time my pregnancy began to get more difficult. Twice, while I slept, I had unexplained bleeding, and had to take a trip to the hospital in the middle of the night.

On my last trip to the emergency room "Shades'" wife flew out to see me. After a 48-hour observation in the hospital, the doctors determined that the baby was healthy and well, but because of the unexplained bleeding they put me on strict bed rest. At that moment "Shades'" wife asked me to come and live with them. She said at their home I wouldn't be alone and would have constant care and anything that I needed. I told her that I couldn't do that, that it would be awkward. She recommended that I come out to Los Angeles with her and that they would put me in an apartment. She said they would pay all my bills, buy all my groceries, and that they would take care of everything. I didn't think I needed all that, but I agreed simply so that I could be closer to "Shades'" wife.

"Shades'" wife put me up in a penthouse hotel suite while she had my apartment professionally packed and all of my things moved to L.A. She then flew me, first class, to my new apartment. And, oh my, was it beautiful. The apartment had spectacular views, the building had a doorman and every amenity and luxury I could ever think of.

When I got there I went to sleep. I was about five and a half months pregnant at that point and I found that I was always tired despite being in the trimester that was supposed to give me so much energy. When I woke up from my nap, "Shades'" wife had ordered a nice dinner and had it delivered to me. I had only been in L.A. for three hours at that point and already it felt like home.

Over the next three months, "Shades'" wife and I shopped like crazy for the baby. She did not want to know the sex of the baby so she bought everything in neutral colors. She'd had the nursery professionally designed and decorated and, out of respect for my feelings, brought me over to see it on a day when "Shades" was out of town at a concert. She had connected me with the best doctors and I hadn't had any more issues for the rest of the pregnancy.

About two weeks before the baby was due, my water broke. I called "Shades'" wife even before I called the doctor. When she got there we called the doctor and he told us to come to the hospital right away.

Although I've always heard horror stories about how long it takes to have one's first child, this baby came right away. I was only in labor for two and a half hours before the baby came out. I gave birth to a beautiful baby girl. She was 7 lbs. 6 oz. and 20 inches long. She had a full head of hair and big beautiful eyes.

When she came out I had the doctor immediately hand her to "Shades'" wife. I expected to feel sadness and sorrow at handing over a child I had carried for so long, but all I felt was total love as I watched "Shades'" wife hold her daughter. About an hour later "Shades" finally got back into town and was able to see the baby. He just held her and kissed her and a tear fell from his eye as he stated, "She looks just like my mother."

I knew from the tabloids even before I met "Shades" that his mom had died right before he made it big. So she had never gotten the chance to see his success. They asked me if it was okay if they named the baby after his mom. I felt honored that they asked my permission but I reminded them that this was their baby.

After two days in the hospital I left and went back to my apartment. The apartment felt empty but not because the baby wasn't there, it was because "Shades'" wife wasn't there. I wasn't expecting a visit from her because I knew she would be busy with the baby, but I must admit that I did miss her. She reminded me a lot of my own mom, and during the time that I was pregnant I really enjoyed having her around.

About two weeks after I gave birth to the baby, "Shades'" wife came to see me. She looked a little tired, but beautiful as always. She happily complained that the baby was keeping them up all night and had such a strong set of lungs that she and "Shades" thought the baby would be the next superstar. She spoke of her with such love and adoration that I knew I had made the right decision.

I ordered us some lunch (strictly salad for me since I was trying to lose the baby weight) and we ate and talked for a while, like old times. Because she didn't want to be away from the baby too long she didn't stay very long but she did have a gift for me. She told me not to open it until she had left. I told her that she didn't have to buy me a gift, but she insisted that I "deserved this" and reiterated that I should not open it until she had left.

When she left I went downstairs to the gym and worked out for a little while and when I came back I started to clean up and cook, so I had forgotten about the gift. As I was getting ready for bed that night I remembered the gift and ran to get it and open it. The gift consisted of an envelope. I expect a first class ticket somewhere because I knew "Shades" and his wife always traveled in style.

In the envelope was a letter from "Shades'" wife. The letter thanked me for making her family complete, for being such a wonderful woman, and for coming into her life and "enriching it." I was so moved by the words in that letter that I found my hands shaking as I read it. At the bottom of the letter was the line "You deserve this and so much more. We love you." I held that letter to my chest and just closed my eyes, relishing in the words "We love you." Sammi had been the only person to say those words to me since the death of my parents, and seeing those words again touched something inside of me.

When I looked back down into the envelope to see what it was that "Shades'" wife had decided that "I deserved' I just gasped. In the envelope was a check for $500,000 with a Post-it note attached. The Post-it note said "This is not payment for the baby, but a thank you for providing such an invaluable service to us." I was speechless and stunned. I didn't know it at the time, but I was destined to go on to provide the same "invaluable service" to many more couples.

Chapter 5: The Second Couple: The Demanding Actress

Over the next two years I was back in fighting form. I had lost all the weight fairly quickly and there were no signs that I'd ever been pregnant, except for slightly fuller breasts that didn't go away. Although I had no complaints about my breasts before the pregnancy, I must admit that I did like their new fullness. They made me look more like a woman.

I had also resumed my social and professional life, but neither were showing any promise. I had gone on several dates but none of them were anyone I would want to be serious with. I hate to stereotype, but I noticed that the men in L.A. were very fickle. Not that I was looking for a man, but some companionship would've been nice.

In my professional life I was having the same difficulty. The club promoting business had its ups and downs. On the one hand it was exciting and fast-paced and there was the opportunity to make really good money. On the other hand it was very risky and there was the chance that you could lose it all just as quickly.

Plus, I was doing it alone. Sammi and I were no longer each other's accomplices. Instead of club promoting she was now happily married and had settled on a regular nine to five. She no longer wanted to be a part of the nightlife, and I can't say that I blamed her. She and her husband had bought a beautiful home, and when I had gone to visit her in Las Vegas I could tell that they were in love. I was happy for her, even though she and I didn't have the same relationship as we'd had before. The truth is, we were in two different phases of life and had grown apart.

I was still living in L.A. because I had grown accustomed to the beautiful weather and all the luxuries that it afforded. I loved L.A. even though I had no real friends there. "Shades'" wife was the closest thing I had to a friend, and I only saw her every blue moon, but I knew it was because she was busy with the baby. I also think a small part of it was that she didn't really want to share her experiences with the baby with me. I understood that and had no hard feelings. I think if I were in her shoes I wouldn't want a constant reminder of my child's biological mother every day either.

Since I had not seen or spoken to "Shades'" wife in a long time, I was surprised when she called me out of the blue one day and asked me out to lunch. She said she had an opportunity for me.

My money had been getting low, and since L.A. was such an expensive place to live, I had started trying to act. I got myself an agent and read a couple scripts and went to a few auditions. I figured if the club promoting thing didn't work, like it hadn't so far, I could fall back on acting, especially since it seemed like everyone was acting these days. At the very least I thought I could get a couple commercials.

When "Shades'" wife called me up, I had thought it was because she had a hookup on a possible movie role for me, or a commercial. "Shades" and his wife were industry big-wigs and I knew they could give me a hookup.

We met for lunch on a Friday afternoon, and after catching up on each other's lives, "Shades'" wife got right to the business at hand. She said she had an unusual request for me, and before I automatically said no she wanted me to hear her out.

I was very intrigued. I listened as "Shades'" wife told me how much she appreciated me giving her the gift of her daughter. She said she couldn't imagine life without her, and that she often bragged to close friends who knew about her infertility that a surrogate had changed her life when she gave her a daughter. She said she had called me a "surrogate" because she didn't want to go into details about how we actually met.

I listened intently as "Shades'" wife told me her story. She said that one day about a month prior, a very good friend of hers had asked to come over. Her friend had said that she had something to say to her and needed to make sure they would be alone. She had assured her friend that "Shades" was out-of-town and that they would be alone except for the housekeeper, but that she would make sure they had total privacy.

When her friend got to the house "Shades'" wife could see that she had been crying. Her friend was fidgety and obviously very nervous. Her friend confided in her that her husband wanted a second child but that she was nervous she would ruin her figure (she was an actress).

Her friend told her about all the surgical procedures she'd had to get her body back after their first child. She talked about how regular diet and exercise along with her personal trainer had helped her lose some weight but didn't give her the body that she wanted - the body that she *needed* if she wanted to keep her career intact.

Her friend told her how nervous she had been going under the knife. "Shades'" wife told me that she was shocked because she had known her friend for quite some time and although she knew she'd already had a daughter she hadn't known that she'd had so much trouble getting the weight off.

In conclusion, her friend told her that she wanted to give her husband a second child but that she did not want to risk her health, her career, and even possibly her life to carry another child. Then her friend asked her if she wouldn't mind putting her in touch with the person she had used as her surrogate.

"Shades'" wife told her friend that she wouldn't mind, they talked for a little bit longer, and then she left. Then "Shades'" wife said to me, "But honestly I wasn't sure if I wanted to do that. I wasn't sure if I wanted to share my 'surrogate' with anyone else." "Shades'" wife quietly said to me, "See, the issue is, they all think you're just a hired surrogate. But I'm fearful that if someone works with you they are going to find out that you were really "Shades'" mistress. I do not want them to know that."

I was surprised to hear "Shades'" wife say this to me. I was surprised to hear the lack of confidence coming from her. To me she always seemed so poised, and sure of herself, that I had trouble thinking of her in any other way. I was so caught up on the vulnerability that I could hear coming from "Shades'" wife's voice, that it took me a while to even process that she had just asked me to be a surrogate for her friend.

My natural reaction was to say "No." Actually, my natural reaction was to say, "Hell no! Why in the world would I intentionally carry someone else's baby?" But I did not say that to "Shades'" wife because I respected her too much and because she'd asked me to keep an open mind about it. So even though my natural reaction was to say "Hell no" I did give it some thought.

To help her case, "Shades'" wife discussed with me how much of an impact I had on her and "Shades'" life. How without me they never would've had their daughter.

She said that I was a life-changer. And that touched something inside of me. But I still had reservations.

For one, I had not set out to become a surrogate. I had not set out to even get pregnant in the first place. But since I had become pregnant, giving the baby to "Shades" and his wife had seemed to be best for the baby, and that was the only reason I had made the decision to do that.

There was a difference in this situation though. Whereas "Shades" and his wife could not have a baby, this person simply did not want to get fat. There was something very vain about that. And for some reason, I felt like if I had agreed to carry this child it would almost be like prostitution. I explained that to "Shades'" wife and she said she could understand my hesitation. But she told me how great a mom this person was. How wonderful she was with the daughter she already had. How much love, kindness, and care she showed to her daughter.

This person had also had older children that she had adopted, and she had been just as wonderful to them as well. "Shades'" wife told me not to look at it as her just not wanting to get fat. She explained how as a professional actress her body was her livelihood. And that it was not an act of vanity so much as of professional necessity. "Shades'" wife's words rang a bell.

As a professional myself, in the male-dominated world of club promotion, I understood how women were limited. A pregnant woman could not and should not promote clubs. No one would want to see her there, and if she was there she would automatically be perceived as a bad mom. Or a bad mom-to-be.

I know that I had never seen a pregnant female club promoter before, and that was part of the reason Sammi had left the business, because she knew she wanted to start a family someday. And she didn't see herself being able to do that as a club promoter.

Still, I didn't think I was totally convinced, so "Shades'" wife suggested I meet her friend and see how she interacted with her daughter before I made up my mind. I agreed and "Shades'" wife said she would call her to see when she was available to meet.

The next day "Shades'" wife called me to see if I was available two weeks from today. And since I was, she set the date for us to meet.

Instead of going to lunch, "Shades'" wife's friend invited us to her home. Before then, "Shades'" wife had not told me who this person was. And oddly enough I did not think to ask. When "Shades'" wife called me to give me the address as well as to tell me who she was, I was shocked.

I had seen a great many of this person's movies, and never thought that I'd be sitting at her home one day discussing having her child. Her husband was also a famous rocker, and he would be there as well.

I arrived at one o'clock, and when I got there I could see "Shades'" wife's car in the circular drive. I got out of my car, went to the door, rang the bell and was greeted by what appeared to be the actress' butler. He showed me into what appeared to be a great room and that is when I saw "Shades'" wife and "The Actress".

I knew she was a slightly older lady simply because I'd seen about 20 years' worth of her movies, but to see her in person you would have never thought she was a day over 21. She was beautiful with milky smooth skin and vibrantly colored hair. Her accent was slight, but it gave a beautiful quality to her voice.

Her husband was there by her side, and appeared to be really laid back, yet personable. "The Actress" on the other hand, seemed timid as she greeted me, and I instantly felt out of place. I don't know if it was because she was a certified B-list actress (she used to be an A-lister in her heyday, and still had a dedicated audience), or because the way she was looking at me made me feel as if I was doing something wrong. I chalked it up to this being her first time making such a request, and tried to make myself feel more comfortable.

As we were talking, a little girl bounded down the stairs, shot across the room, and jumped into "The Actress'" arms, with a handful of crayons. Despite the fact that

"The Actress" was dressed in all white, she hugged the little girl wholeheartedly. Both she and the little girl's faces were lit up as "The Actress" introduced me to her daughter. The little girl sat quietly on her lap as we continued our conversation.

I watched the little girl. She seemed so comfortable in her mom's arms. She alternated between playing with her mom's fingers and twisting her mom's hair between her own little fingers. At one point she started to close her eyes and drift off to sleep, and her mom excused herself from our conversation so that she could lay her daughter down for a nap.

I was pleasantly surprised at this gesture. Considering "The Actress'" level of celebrity, I had assumed she would have a nanny come and get her daughter to take her for a nap. Although "The Actress" had initially made me feel ill at ease, the love that she had for her daughter helped make up my mind. I knew that if I became her surrogate, that the child that I carried for her would have a loving home and a loving family.

We finished up lunch, and then I told "The Actress" and her husband that I would let them know what my decision was very soon. On the way out to our cars, I whispered to "Shades'" wife that I would do it. I said that I would be a surrogate for this couple. "Shades'" wife gave me a big hug and told me that she would call her friend this evening and give her the great news.

A couple days later "The Actress", "Shades'" wife, and I, all met up to hash out the details. "Shades'" wife's friend had me sign a NDA, which is a Nondisclosure Agreement stating that I would not disclose the details of our surrogacy arrangement. Before that I had never heard of an NDA.

The plan was for me to meet with "The Actress'" own personal doctor and be impregnated through in vitro fertilization using "The Actress'" eggs and her husband's sperm. The procedure was to take place in one month during which time I was to begin taking folic acid supplements.

"The Actress" imposed a few restrictions, and asked that I not smoke or drink or consume caffeine during the pregnancy. I didn't smoke, and wasn't a big coffee drinker anyway, so that wasn't a problem. As far as alcohol, I already knew not to drink while pregnant, so that wasn't a problem either.

After I had signed everything and we had discussed all the particulars, then came the part about compensation. Prior to this meeting, "Shades'" wife had asked me what I wanted to be paid for this. I had no idea. I had never done this before. And although "Shades'" wife had given me half a million dollars for carrying her child, neither of us knew if that would be a good number. So I decided to leave the number open. I would let "The Actress" make an offer. So when we got to that part I was noticeably quiet.

"The Actress", despite seeming shy and timid to me, boldly wrote the number that she proposed paying me on a sheet of paper, and just like if we were in a movie, slid it across the table to me.

Although I was pleasantly surprised when I saw the number, I tried to play it off. I took a sip of my tea, and acted as if that number was no big deal. After looking at the number for a couple minutes - because I didn't want to appear too anxious - I then signed on the dotted line. The number, by the way, was $1 million. "The Actress" and her husband were going to pay me $1 million to be their surrogate!

On the outside I was quiet and poised, but on the inside I was screaming! One million dollars was enough to restore a lot of the money I had originally had, and get me close to where I had started, despite all the failed business attempts and haphazard ways in which I had initially spent my inheritance.

Combined with the six figures I currently had left in my bank account, this money would give me the opportunity to make some wiser decisions and better investments. I felt like I was being given an opportunity to start all over again. And so began my journey with couple number two.

I started IVF with couple number two one month later. The month gave me time to take folic acid and to get myself ready for the next 10 months. After taking folic acid I went to see "The Actress'" fertility doctor to begin IVF. The implantation "took" on the second go-round and almost three months from the day we had our first meeting at "The Actress'" house we found out I was pregnant.

Unlike the first time around (two times if you count my pregnancy in college), I got sick feeling right away. I felt nauseous and my breasts felt so tender I could not sleep on them. And I was so tired. I would literally wake up in the morning, brush my teeth, get nauseous, force down a couple crackers, throw up, and go back to bed. I did this for nearly 10 days until my next appointment with "The Actress" and her doctor.

The morning of the appointment "The Actress" sent her car to pick me up. She wanted us to ride to the doctor appointment together. I don't know if it was because she wanted to make sure her baby arrived safely, or if it was because she wanted to "catch up" with me on the way there.

Either way, when the car got there and my doorman alerted me to come down, as I got in the car, "The Actress" started to give me the once over. She checked out everything from my pedicure (which was old and hadn't been refreshed in about three weeks) to my clothes (which were wrinkled), to my hair (which looked tired, like I felt). I don't even think she noticed it, but she frowned slightly as she assessed me and I could see her displeasure.

Because I was in a bad mood - throwing up all day can do that to a person - I just turned away from her and looked out of the window. After we had driven a few blocks, I turned back to look at her and she was still checking me out.

As I began to turn away again, I heard her mumble, "You've lost some weight." I ignored her and turned back to the window. Before we could get to the doctor's office, which was only a couple miles away, I was already asleep. This pregnancy was already giving me a run for the money.

"The Actress'" doctor was an older man who looked like he'd seen it all. After he checked me out, he confirmed that I had indeed lost a good deal of weight (about 15 pounds). Unlike my "employer," however, he was not overly concerned. He assured her that it was not uncommon for some women to lose weight in the beginning of their pregnancy, and that no matter what, the baby would still get what it needed nutrition-wise, even if I didn't. To be sure, he prescribed multivitamins to me along with plenty of rest.

After the appointment "The Actress" offered to take me to lunch. I declined because I was so tired. She dropped me back off at my place and I immediately went back to sleep. I had been sleeping for three maybe four hours when my doorman rang my phone. I groggily answered the phone, and he informed me that I had a package. I told him to send it up.

When I got to the door and opened it, all I could do was stand there in complete and utter amazement. Standing outside of my door was food delivered from every type of restaurant one could think of. There was Chinese food, Soul food, French food, Fast food, and Italian food.

Behind the people carrying the food was a three person team who informed me they were there to give me a full service spa treatment, including a chemical-less manicure, pedicure, and massage. Without even looking at the card that accompanied the vast array of food, I knew that all this was from "The Actress". I excitedly let everyone into my apartment.

While they were setting up, I read the card that accompanied the package. It read simply, "For Baby." I was surprised to find that I was actually hungry, so I dove in. I sampled everything there, and even went back for seconds. When I was done devouring my food, I sat back and prepared for my mani-pedi.

After the manicure and pedicure, I received a light massage, and then the team left. The people dropping off the food had already left, so I found myself alone.

Without meaning to, I began to cry. I don't know if it was because I felt lonely, or if it was the hormones, but I couldn't stop crying. I decided to take a walk and go get some fresh air. While on my walk, I stopped by a local flower shop and bought some fresh flowers to put on my table. And that's when it hit me. I was missing my parents. My mom used to put fresh flowers on the table every Saturday afternoon. I had inadvertently grabbed flowers to bring back home with me. The gesture made me smile, and made me feel like mom was there with me.

Another thought plagued me, however. I wondered what mom would think of my new "career" as a celebrity surrogate. When I was a teenager, and often went to mom complaining that I was flat-chested and boring-looking, she would reassure me that everything about me was beautifully made and would serve a purpose - even my so-called plain jane-ness. Looking back, I somehow doubted that she thought my purpose would become the nondescript child-bearer for celebrities.

Although I thought mom might be displeased, I reasoned that she would never judge me and loved me no matter what. Then I quickly put the matter out of my mind. It was too hard to think about.

When I entered the second trimester of pregnancy, my energy returned. I had my checkup, and like she always did, "The Actress" accompanied me and we rode there together. After the checkup, the doctor cleared me and confirmed for "The Actress" how far along I was, that way she wouldn't schedule any movies around the time that I was to give birth. She seemed pleased with my progress and happy that things were going according to plan.

During the second trimester, now that we were "out of danger" "The Actress" began to get more difficult. She had shed that seemingly shy and reserved persona and had begun to make demands and requests. Because she was my "employer," I obliged wherever I could. For example, whereas she used to send me a variety of foods, she now sent only organic. She was particular about what I ate and had begun to send over the day's meal – carefully selected - every day. She also started insisting that I take small walks. I didn't mind, because I figured it would be easier to lose the weight if I stayed active.

But then the demands grew. "The Actress" became downright controlling. She had already taken control of my menu and my physical activity, but then she began sending me classical music to play to my belly/her baby. I obliged. As I began to grow bigger in size, she sent over a housekeeper to "straighten up." I immediately called her and thanked her. I thought that was very thoughtful. It took me awhile to realize this "housekeeper" was actually her spy. She was using the housekeeper to keep an eye on me.

Like the time when the housekeeper was cleaning my refrigerator, and the next day I got a call from "The Actress" asking me if I needed anything. I said, "No, I'm fine." And as we were getting off the phone she threw in a question about whether I had drank any alcohol during the pregnancy. I said, "No, of course not," and we got off the phone. That whole day I had been trying to figure out why she had asked me a random question like that. I just couldn't figure it out.

That evening when I went into the refrigerator to get a snack, I saw a handwritten sign that the housekeeper had left on a bottle of wine that was in my refrigerator. The sign said, "Shall I discard this?" That's when I knew where that seemingly random question had come from.

For one, the bottle of wine had been in my refrigerator since before I was pregnant, and secondly, I didn't appreciate the housekeeper snooping then relaying information back to "The Actress". The next day I made sure to call "The Actress" and "randomly" slip in that I had an old bottle of wine in the fridge, and that I was wondering if the housekeeper might like it. She sheepishly responded that that was so sweet of me to offer it to the housekeeper, but that she made sure none of her employees consumed alcohol. As if the previous signs weren't enough confirmation, that comment let me know for sure that "The Actress" was a control freak.

Another time the housekeeper snooped on me was when I'd had a male visitor (actually it was my insurance guy) and the next day "The Actress" called me up to "chit-chat" and "see how I was doing" and within five minutes had worked into the conversation questions about "if I was seeing anyone" or "if I frequently had male visitors." I told her that I was not seeing anyone, and because I was growing frustrated with her constant prying into my personal life, I sarcastically told her that when I started seeing someone she would be the third to know. And then came her reply.

Without missing a beat, she told me that in the event that I did start to see someone she would prefer that I not engage in sexual activity for the duration of my pregnancy. I was shocked. I mean, shocked to the point of speechlessness.

I wasn't so much shocked that she would want me to refrain from sexual activity while I carried her baby. It was a common misconception that having sex while pregnant could harm or otherwise affect a baby. I, too, had wondered about that while pregnant with "Shades'" baby. I had since then learned, however, that a developing baby is not harmed during sex – assuming the pregnancy was uncomplicated.

Still, I could see where she was coming from with that. My shock was that she had the audacity to ask me that, to make such a request in the first place. But she didn't stop there.

The hits just kept coming with this lady. Her housekeeper began removing "harmful" items from my place, without my permission. Though I'd be willing to bet that she had the permission of "The Actress".

For example, all my hair dyes suddenly disappeared and were replaced by a "surprise" visit from "The Actress'" personal hairstylist. "The Actress" sent her personal hairstylist to my home with a note that said "I just wanted to do something nice for you. I am hoping a beautiful new hairstyle will be a complement to your natural glow." Yeah right, I thought. The only thing she was hoping was that I wouldn't dye my own hair and hurt the baby.

I wanted to remind her that I had done this before. And that I wasn't a total idiot. I wanted to assure her that I would never dye my hair while I was pregnant. But what I did instead was just enjoy my luxurious, in-home hair appointment. Oh, and when I was done getting my hair done, I fired her housekeeper. Take that.

Although "The Actress" would've never told me so, I figured I must have been doing something right, and that she was bragging about me, because before I had even gotten to my eighth month I'd already had two more couples call me up and asked me to be a surrogate for them.

I was excited in spite of myself. I had never intended to become a celebrity surrogate, but it was very profitable, and I thought that I had made a good move.

I mean, I didn't mind being pregnant. Aside from a little bit of sickness at the beginning of this pregnancy, I felt very normal. I had even been given a free "pregnancy-induced" breast job as a result of my first pregnancy, or second pregnancy depending on if you counted the one that I had with Eddie. Whenever I thought about that first pregnancy I got very sad, so I erased that thought.

I asked "Shades'" wife to accompany me to my meetings with these two couples, but I don't think she wanted to be affiliated with celebrity surrogacy. I don't think she wanted too many people to know how her own daughter had gotten here, so without coming right out and saying it to me, she just slowly but surely exited out of my life.

"Shades'" wife gradually stopped returning phone calls, she stopped replying to text messages, and at some point I read in the news that she and "Shades" had moved. I also read that she and "Shades" were expecting their second child and I hoped it was true. Although I obviously don't think anything is wrong with surrogacy, I hoped that she was finally able to get pregnant and give "Shades" the son he wanted. She had been my one remaining friend and I truly wanted the best for her. Even if it meant I no longer fit into her life.

So without "Shades'" wife to accompany me, I went to an attorney to receive some guidance about how to proceed with becoming an official surrogate for celebrities. The attorney drew up some contracts for me to have ready for my new "celebrity clients" to sign. So that now, along with their NDA, I too had an NDA, as well as a contract that protected my interests.

For example, one part of my contract stated that the celebrity in question would, in fact, take receipt of their child and not change their mind. After all, we all know that celebrities can sometimes be fickle.

I had a contract drawn out for what I would be paid and how the funds would be received. The attorney also advised me to get an official contact number. I thought since this was a discrete business I shouldn't do that, but my attorney assured me that I could keep the number discrete and still provide a way for the celebrities to contact me to arrange the initial meeting and to secure the surrogacy services.

I did all those things and before I knew it I was officially in business. Because of the NDAs that are still current with some of my celebrity clients, and because doing so might indicate who I am, I will not say what my company name used to be. Revealing my former company's name might violate the NDA, and by default, identify many of my former clients. And trust me, they would not be happy about that. Most of them already will be pissed that I've told this much, though they'll never admit that it's them I'm talking about.

After I was "legalized" and formally in business, I set up a meeting with the first person. By now, I had learned that it was common to not know the name of the celebrity until the last minute. So, it didn't surprise me when I was given a meeting place and time without knowing who I was meeting.

I got there late, as I always seemed to do these days. It was hectic carrying around the extra weight, and most recently my back had started to hurt and my feet were swelling, so moving in general was an effort.

About twenty minutes past the time we were supposed to meet, I got to the location. It was the restaurant of an expensive hotel. I wondered why a celebrity who obviously wanted to maintain discretion would set up a meeting in such a public place.

Whatever the reason, I used the fact that we were in a restaurant to order myself some food. I was hungry most of the time as of late, especially since I was unable to eat too much at one time. I ordered a steak and steamed asparagus, and then I nervously started to look around.

Over the months of working with "The Actress" I had come to know that she could be incredibly resourceful, and like a true mom, she seemed to have eyes and ears in the back of her head. She had explicitly "forbidden" red meat from my diet (I guess she didn't want me to give the newborn a heart attack), but I think the fact that she had forbidden it made me want it even more. It is never a good idea to deny a pregnant woman food. Ever.

Anyway, when the 9 oz. steak arrived, I dove into it and didn't even look up again until I had eaten several pieces. When I did look up I was surprised to see a very famous socialite standing just outside the door of the restaurant signing autographs. I nearly choked on my steak when I saw who it was.

This person was a very wealthy socialite who had become famous for doing nothing in particular. At one point she had been on a popular television show, and before that she had made a career out of simply partying.

It had briefly occurred to me that she might be there to meet me, that she might be the celebrity who was interested in hiring a surrogate. But before that thought could completely enter my mind I quickly dismissed it.

This was not the type of person who wanted to be tied down with a child. Still, I enjoyed seeing this celebrity, especially since her fame had somewhat faded and sightings of her had become a bit of a rarity these days.

As I inhaled my steak, I watched this person make her rounds. She posed for pictures, she signed autographs, all while laughing and joking with the paparazzi.

With the way she was soaking up the attention, if I didn't know any better, I would've thought she had called the paparazzi there. But I sat there enjoying the show nonetheless, wondering who else I would see come through this popular hotel.

As I sat there finishing my steak, and of course dessert, I did in fact see a couple more celebrities come through the door. There was a famous basketball player surrounded by his entourage. And a female singer, dressed to the nines, walked by with another lady talking quickly into her ear. I assumed the lady was her publicist and that she was there for a photo shoot.

Watching for celebrity sightings was so interesting, that I didn't notice that I had been waiting there for over an hour. By then "The Socialite" and the paparazzi were gone. I summoned my waiter, preparing to ask him for my check so I could get out of there. When he came over he informed me that my bill had already been paid. It took me a minute to realize that I had been stood up. I wondered if the person had seen me and changed their mind about me being a surrogate for them, or if they had changed their mind before seeing me but had decided to at least pay my bill as a condolence.

In any case, I arose to leave and as I went to stand at the valet table to retrieve my car, a stretch limo pulled up to me. I looked around to see if there was someone standing behind me, and there was no one. Then the back window rolled down. I immediately thought that it was "The Actress" coming to snoop on me or out me for eating red meat. But I was surprised to see that it was "The Socialite".

"The Socialite" called me by my "work" name, and asked if I wouldn't mind conducting our business in the car. Because she knew the code name, I knew she was the person I had been waiting for, so I got into the vehicle. When the door closed behind us, there she was - "The Socialite" - in person.

In the backseat of this stretch limo was "The Socialite", a young man, and two little dogs that wouldn't stop chirping at me. I would say barking, but they were so little that I didn't think that they could bark. The noises actually sounded like little chirps. "The Socialite" looked me over, and then asked me if I was hungry or thirsty. Considering that I just ate I was neither. And since "The Socialite" had paid for my meal I knew that she knew that. I figured her offering to feed me, again, was her attempt to break the ice. Maybe she thought that pregnant women ate every hour on the hour.

I could see that she was a bit uncomfortable with my very pregnant body. She kept staring at my belly as if she thought that at any minute whatever was in it would jump out and bite her. The baby was moving and shifting at that point, courtesy of the meal I had just eaten, so I told her she could touch my belly if she'd like. She looked at it almost in disgust and declined. I thought that was pretty weird considering that we were there to discuss the possibility of me carrying a child for her.

Then I thought maybe there was an explanation. Maybe she was meeting me to screen me for someone else. But sure enough, within a couple minutes of me getting into the limo, she told me she wanted a baby.

"The Socialite" said that she had always wanted to be a young mom, so that she could be cool and stylish with her daughter. She said she did not particularly want to be married, and she didn't want to wait around to find some perfect guy, that she had already kissed enough frogs to know that the perfect guy didn't exist.

I had no problem with any of those points. Although personally I thought that it was better to have two people raising a child than one, I did not care that she wasn't married. I knew that things happened and that even if someone started out as a couple, they could easily split up or divorce and still raise a child alone. Plus, given the amount of money this person had, she could easily afford to raise the child on her own, and probably would have more help available to her than even a two-parent household. On a personal note, I also thought marriage was overrated and outdated (even though I secretly still hoped to experience it myself one day), so her being unmarried didn't bother me.

What did bother me, however, was the fact that this person apparently wanted a baby but seemed grossed out by my pregnant belly and uninterested in even touching the baby that was growing inside me. I decided I wouldn't judge her by that. I thought that maybe she was grossed out by my pregnant belly, much in the same way that a person who hasn't been pregnant before might be before they actually experienced it for themselves.

I was a perfect example. Before getting pregnant, as a teenager, the sight of pregnant people had always made me feel uncomfortable. They looked so swollen and uncomfortable. And I thought they smelled funny. But I was a teenager and didn't know any better then.

Even though this person was older and should've known better, I figured she was just uncomfortable with the situation because it was unfamiliar. I also thought that maybe she didn't want to touch my belly because the baby growing inside wasn't hers. I again figured that when it was her baby that she'd be interested in at least touching and connecting with it.

We rode along further and "The Socialite" poured drink after drink as she talked to me about her own childhood. I wasn't too happy about the drinking, but figured she was nervous.

She discussed what appeared to be a very privileged childhood with a staff built completely around her. She said that she wanted to give her daughter every advantage she had been given and would hire a team of people to make sure that happened. That was another red flag considering that she talked as if she herself wouldn't be involved.

Despite my effort to not judge this person based on what I had read about her in the press and even some of the things I was seeing with my own eyes, I had to admit that the whole conversation gave me a funny feeling. To say I was uncomfortable would be putting it mildly. Something about her was rubbing me the wrong way, and in my heart of hearts I knew that this person was not ready for a child. I asked more questions in an attempt to learn more about her. I thought learning more about her would allow me to see her beyond the surface. I was trying to get at the heart of who she was.

What I learned shocked me. After about seven drinks, she finally opened up that a friend of hers had gotten pregnant and that although it had been an accident, the friend had managed to gain more popularity and turn the "mistake" into press and media exposure. She said she needed to be able to compete and having children was the next big thing. I literally gasped when she said that. I would have loved to have her laugh and say, "I was just kidding!" But the buzzed socialite didn't even crack a smile. She then went on to ask me if I would be available to be a nanny to the child after I had delivered it. She said she would pay any amount of money, "just name my price."

I sat there flabbergasted, which I think she took to mean that I was in agreement. She started going on and on about whether I would supply the sperm or if she should, and if she supplied the sperm would I want to have sex with the person she chose or should he deliver it in a cup? The whole time I am sitting there in complete shock and awe, and with growing anger.

After a moment of silence (on my part), I asked for the driver to pull over. The clueless socialite asked me if I was going to hurl. I ignored her because given her ignorance and my hormones, I feared I might reach across the limo and strangle her.

When the limo stopped and I got out, "The Socialite" loudly asked me what I was doing. I replied, as calmly as I could muster, "I wouldn't carry a child for you for any money in the world," and proceeded to walk away. She yelled at me that she would find someone else, and called me a Bit@h! I walked away as fast as my legs could carry me.

As angry as I was, especially at being called the "B" word, I was more upset that this person could (and probably would) hire someone to bring a child into this world for her. And rich or not, no child deserved a mother like that. At one point – from what I read in the press - I think this person had even managed to lose her dog (and that appeared to be the only thing that "The Socialite" did care about, other than herself).

Even though I hadn't prayed since the night of my parents' accident, I said a quick prayer then and there that this person would not have a child nor hire anyone to carry a child for her anytime soon. Then I hailed a cab to get back to my car and get home.

This had been a long day, and even though this would be the first time I would turn down a celebrity seeking a surrogate, it certainly would not be the last.

One week later I met with the second couple who had contacted me about being a surrogate for them.

Unlike the other couples, I knew who this person was right away, as she had asked me to meet them at her husband's property.

When I got to the property, it was everything I expected of someone of this caliber. This person, who I'll call "Richie Rich", was by far the wealthiest of any of the clients I'd had so far. And he wanted everyone around him to know it. I was invited to his property, in my opinion, just so that I would see how rich he truly was.

From day one, everything he did was a power play. He kept me waiting for him for an hour even though I was nearly nine months pregnant. When I did get to the office, he wasn't in there, and I had to sit there and wait some more.

I used that time as an opportunity to look around (which I'm sure he wanted me to do) and I couldn't help but admire the sheer opulence of his surroundings. I will not go into detail about what was in the office, as I might inadvertently reveal something that I should not. What I will say is that his office alone probably cost more than most people make in a lifetime.

Needless to say, I was sufficiently impressed and intimated. I hated that I was, because I know that's what he was going for by making me wait, but I was. When he walked into the room, it was without his wife. The first thing he said to me was, "Good. You're not fat. I don't like fat people. It implies that one doesn't have self- control. And being pregnant is no excuse to get fat or to lose control." His words were as bold and boisterous as he was. After he said what he said he looked at me as if he was waiting for me to get offended. As if he was daring me to say something.

I couldn't tell if those words were said because he meant them or because he wanted to get a rise out of me. Probably a little bit of both. In any case, I knew then and there that I was dealing with a different kind of person. It's true that celebrities (many, if not most) expect to get what they want. But this person was the worst type of celebrity. He was powerful, rich, and depended on no one to ensure his wealth. This made him the most arrogant of celebrities because unlike movie stars and performers who depended on being liked and respected by "the people," this person did not. "The people" aren't who made him rich, and had nothing to do with him being successful. As such, being liked or respected was insignificant to him.

On the contrary, he seemed to like being disliked. It was like he got off on it. After he didn't get a reaction out of me, he proceeded to tell me what he needed. He stated that although he had several grown children, he wished to expand his bloodline and have a child with his new wife. He was very direct in stating that neither she nor he wished her to lose her figure, so they were in the market for a surrogate. He stated that he wanted discretion and he wanted the best. Then he cast his eyes on me like it was somehow time for me to show that I was the best.

For some reason, his was the only interview where I felt like I was applying for the job of being his surrogate. With others, of course they were evaluating me as much as I was evaluating them, but with him it seemed like he was somehow trying to decide if he would bestow upon me the honor of being his celebrity surrogate.

As if on cue, and because he was staring at me expectantly, I began to tell him a little about what I did, how surrogacy worked, and what the expectations were. He cut me off somewhere around my spiel about contracts and NDAs to ask me for some of the names of my previous (and current) clients. I explained to him that I operated discreetly and protected the anonymity of my clients and did not disclose that information. He told me to cut the crap and tell him who my last few clients had been.

I repeated that my NDAs prevented me from doing that. He seemed to take that as a personal challenge, leaned in, and whispered that he could keep a secret better than most and that if I did not tell him he would not give me the job. I flinched but remained firm and told him that I did not and would not disclose that information, even if it meant losing out on a job. He told me that if I was stupid enough to walk away from 2.5 million dollars, then I was too stupid to be a surrogate for him.

I flinched again, but this time it was from a combination of the harsh way he spoke to me and the realization that I would be turning down a 2.5 million dollar payday. I must have blinked a million times as my mind tried to sort through what was going on and figure out what I should do.

On the one hand, I could keep the information secret and honor the NDAs, and lose out on a hefty payday in the process. Or I could tell this one individual, with no one around, swear him to secrecy, rely on him being honorable, and make a lot of money.

It took me five seconds to make up my mind. I stood up, shook the hand of this imposing and intimidating figure, told him it had been a pleasure to meet him, and prepared to leave. Although I had hoped he would stop me, he did not, and I was escorted from his property like a common thief.

I was sad to lose that job. Even though this person had appeared to be a complete "a-hole" and jerk, I knew how much he loved and protected his children. I knew that he already was a great father, and would have been a great parent to the child I carried for him. He was very much a keep-it-in-the-family kind of man, and shared all of his wealth and business savvy with his children. He had even been very kind to his ex-wives, so I knew he was a man that both loved and protected his family.

If given the chance, indeed it would have been an honor to surrogate for him. Since I had essentially been fired by him for not disclosing the names of my former clients, and since I had decided not to work with the selfish, self-centered socialite, I had no couples lined up to surrogate for.

For days I considered stopping at this point, since no one was calling anymore anyway. It all ended a week later when I got a call from a client's representative asking me to meet them for dinner at a super expensive restaurant.

When I got there I was seated in an exclusive and private part of the restaurant away from the other patrons. When I entered the room, lo and behold, there sat "Richie Rich" and his wife. He was smiling ear to ear and actually rose to pull my seat back for me.

When I sat, with what I imagine must've been a confused look on my face, he explained that he had wanted to hire me right away to be a surrogate for he and his wife. He said he admired my integrity and character, and that what happened last week had been a test. He was checking to see if I would be discreet and loyal, even when presented with a huge cash payout.

"Richie Rich" said there was nothing more important than the loyalty, honesty and integrity of a person's word and he was very pleased when I demonstrated that to him at our meeting last week. He said he knew then and there that he would hire me, he had just waited to call me back because he wanted it to be a time when both he and his wife were available.

I smiled when he told me that. Actually, it was more like I blushed. After that first meeting with this man, I didn't know what to expect. But I was pleasantly surprised when he turned out to be incredibly charming and kind. The tough, sarcastic, hothead seemed to be a façade that he had adopted in business. The real "Richie Rich" was sweet and witty, with a great sense of humor and personality. It was no wonder he had landed so many beautiful girlfriends and wives. Of course his money contributed to his appeal, but he was also very charming. He was still arrogant though. But who wasn't? By now, I had met a ton of arrogant celebrities, and had come to realize that getting what they wanted when they wanted it made many of them that way. I don't think they started out that way. It had become an adapted trait.

After we ate dinner, we discussed the terms of the arrangement. In no uncertain terms, "Richie Rich" let me know that he wanted to get this going right away.

Considering that I was in the last several weeks of my current pregnancy, he knew we couldn't start right then, but he wanted us to get "it" done soon. It was obvious that he was used to getting what he wanted when he wanted it. Having had a few babies by now, I knew that things didn't always go as scheduled. For his sake, and mine, however, I hoped things would go as planned.

Exactly four weeks from the day that I met with "Richie Rich" I had "The Actress'" baby. Despite my "no red meat, only lean meats" diet, I managed to deliver a huge baby. The baby was so big that it fractured its collarbone coming out during delivery, not to mention what it did to me. I had to have an episiotomy (surgical procedure repairing the skin torn between the vaginal and anal openings during vaginal delivery) and that meant extra time to heal.

I knew that "Richie Rich" would not be pleased. "The Actress" certainly was not pleased with me. She openly blamed me for having such a big baby. She looked at me skeptically when I told her I had only eaten the foods that she had sent over (I didn't bother telling her that I'd had a few slip-ups, because she wouldn't have believed me anyway and that's not why the baby was so big).

The doctor assured her that the baby was healthy and in a normal weight range, albeit on the high-end, and she reluctantly backed off me. But not until she was assured that a baby being on the "larger side" at birth was no indication that the baby would grow up to become an obese child. I guess given her career field she was already worried about the baby's image. Celebrities never failed to amaze me.

Chapter 6: The Third Couple: Richie Rich

As I expected, it took longer for me to heal. Instead of needing the six weeks that women who delivered vaginally needed, I had to take eight weeks to heal, and I took another eight weeks to give my body time to rest.

The additional weeks it took to heal to anybody other than "Richie Rich" would have been acceptable and perfectly understandable. To "Richie Rich", however, it was anything but. He demanded to know why we were not starting on time, and even when I explained to him why, he was not satisfied with the answer. He called the doctor an idiot, and even went so far as to request a discount since "time was of the essence" and "I could not provide a timely service."

See, that's why rich people stayed rich, because they were so stingy and tight-fisted with their money. And despite having so much money, they fully expected to get any and everything either deeply discounted or free.

I stood my ground (partly because it had worked before and also because I legitimately could not do anything about having to take the extra time) and told "Richie Rich" that I could not discount his surrogacy service, and reiterated that for the health of his child it was best that I be allowed to heal properly.

Normally, it was encouraged for a woman to wait six months to a year, and sometimes two years depending on how she delivered, before she should get pregnant again. But due to the expertise of medical technology, my youth, and partly the impatience of my clients, I was able to (or had to in many cases) move faster. But this was ridiculous to expect that I couldn't have an extra few weeks to recover.

When "Richie Rich" saw that he was not above the rules of pregnancy he backed off, but not before making sure that I knew he was displeased.

In total I took four months off. During that time "Richie Rich" strongly suggested that I move into his property. Because I knew that "Richie Rich" was controlling, and because I'd worked with controlling celebrities in the past, I did not want to move into "Richie Rich's" property. The property was beautiful. And I knew that I would be surrounded in luxury, but I did not think it was worth the headache that I knew would accompany being so close to "Richie Rich's" command. I tried to weasel my way out of it, but because "Richie Rich" had backed off the previous issue he attacked this one with the ferocity of a pit bull. He would not accept no for an answer. So it was decided that I would move into his building. I packed up the necessities, because he had already told me that he would provide everything that I needed, and I moved into his property.

Those four months were something out of a dream. The apartment itself was so beautiful and so luxurious that it took me a week before I even felt comfortable enough to sit on the furniture. I would walk around the apartment looking at everything as if I was in a museum, and not in the place that would be my home for the next year. The views were spectacular, and I found myself being able to think clearly for the first time since the tragic death of my parents.

I found myself wondering about them. Specifically, I was again wondering if they would be pleased. I hated to indulge myself in this kind of thinking, because in all truth I think I knew the answer.

But I couldn't help it. I thought about what it was that my parents had wanted for me, and what I had initially wanted for myself. I never once thought that I would be carrying children for anyone, let alone celebrities. If ever I had planned to carry a child I thought it would be my own.

Once again, I reasoned that no matter what I did my parents would always love and be proud of me. I figured they would understand why I had become a celebrity surrogate. And I figured that they would be proud that I was in control of my own life and fairly successful at my chosen occupation. I knew though that I would not be able to do this forever. And I hoped that I would find a career that would make me happy. And that would make mom and dad proud.

In the meantime, however, I had a job to do. So after the four months of healing and resting were up, we moved full steam ahead to the IVF procedure. Although I had done this procedure a few times before, working with "Richie Rich" was a little different. "Richie Rich" specified that he wanted a boy and was willing to spend any amount of money to make sure that he got a boy. This entailed a procedure in which "Richie Rich's" sperm was separated by x and y chromosomes. The x chromosomes were discarded, leaving only y chromosomes in place, so that he could have a boy.

My, oh my, what money can buy! I had no idea such a procedure existed, let alone what the costs might be. But what I was coming to fully understand was that "Richie Rich" got what "Richie Rich" wanted.

Sure enough, six months into our professional relationship, and only a short two months after my four month break, the IVF took and I became pregnant. "Richie Rich" was so pleased that he bought me a platinum tennis bracelet, and although his wife hadn't done anything at all, he bought her one too. The one he bought her made mine look like a baby tennis bracelet, but I appreciated the gesture because he did not have to buy me anything.

My pregnancy for "Richie Rich" was pretty uneventful except that this was the first pregnancy that I got stretch marks. Even when I delivered "The Actress'" huge baby, I did not get any stretch marks, but this time around they were everywhere.

At only five months pregnant, I had stretch marks on my belly, on my breasts, at the top of my thighs, and on my hips. I was beginning to look like I was wearing a tiger-striped bodysuit and I hated the way my body looked.

In typical "Richie Rich" form, he checked me at least monthly to make sure I wasn't getting overweight. He wanted a healthy baby, but he didn't want a fat woman carrying his baby. Those were his exact words. He warned me that men did not like fat women, and told me on more than one occasion that obesity was a sign of a lack of self-control.

Even though I had thought differently when I first met him, now I thought that as charming as "Richie Rich" could be, for the life of me, sometimes I could not figure out how he managed to marry so many beautiful women. Because even though he could be charming and charismatic, he could also be a prick with absolutely no filter on what he said and no regard for who it might hurt. But then I remembered his money, and answered my own question.

Aside from my stretch marks, and regular "obesity" checks, the pregnancy went by without a hitch. And as obnoxious as "Richie Rich" was, my pregnancy for him was one of the most normal.

I delivered a beautiful, burly, healthy boy on the actual day he was due. "Richie Rich" was pleased, and stated that his new son knew the value of being on time and being a man of his word. I thought that was cute and laughed, but I'm sure that "Richie Rich" was serious.

"Richie Rich's" wife was at the hospital, and to her benefit she looked delighted to have the baby. Although she was dressed in designer from head to toe, she held the baby against her body and in her accent-heavy voice said that he was beautiful. She held him the whole time they were there, except for when he needed to see the doctor for his circumcision and other medical care.

When it was time to change his diaper she jumped at the chance to learn. It was cute watching her try to daintily change a diaper that had been stained with thick, black, newborn-baby poop. But she managed to learn to do it, and she looked supermodel-beautiful as she did it.

"Richie Rich" allowed me to continue to live on his property for as long as I liked. I took him up on the offer for the duration of the six weeks postpartum, but then soon after moved out.

Although "Richie Rich" had been kind in many ways, he had been no nonsense when it came to certain things. The first had been weight gain. Thanks to his obsession with my weight, I had dropped all but five pounds of the weight I'd gained during the pregnancy over the course of my six weeks postpartum rest.

Still, my body was pretty worse for wear. It definitely looked like the body of a woman who'd had children. Other mothers will know what I am talking about. There is a definite look that most of us get when we bear children, and although I was on the thin side, in my opinion, it had become obvious that I had carried a baby (or a few of them). At least it had become obvious to me.

In addition to weight gain, "Richie Rich" had also been no nonsense about me meeting up with prospective clients while I was pregnant with his baby. He had expressly forbidden me to meet with any potential clients while I was pregnant with his baby. He asserted that he had hired me for a job and he wanted my total attention.

I don't know if he thought that by my meeting with other clients it would somehow make me carry less of his baby, or not do it as well, but I just honored his request. By now I was used to celebrity quirks.

Since "Richie Rich" had not let me meet with any new clients while I was a surrogate for him, I had to wait until after I had delivered.

After my six week postpartum wellness check, I decided that it would then be a good time to line up my next client. I had four calls awaiting my response. I noticed that as I did this more and more, my popularity as a trusted celebrity surrogate had gained. Not surprisingly, it had all been by word of mouth. I mean, after all, this is not typically something a person advertises.

Two of the calls I eliminated pretty quickly. One of them was a Saudi prince that wanted me to "make him a son" to carry on his name. His requirements were that I "make his son" at least six feet tall with a lighter complexion because the belief in his culture was that taller men could see an enemy coming and thus avert it (so they were considered lucky) and a lighter complexion was an indication of higher social status.

I did not bother calling this man back to explain that I could not "make" him anything. That I was simply the shell - the figurative oven - and that the child I carried for him would be from his own seed/sperm, and usually from the egg of his partner. I didn't bother explaining that because I would have declined the job anyway since the Saudi prince wanted me to live in his country, which I was not willing to do.

The second call came from an independently wealthy, high-powered lesbian couple that wanted to use their own eggs, but they wanted me to find them some "celebrity" sperm for their unborn child. They even had a list naming some of the celebrities they would "consider."

I did not call them back to explain that I was not a sperm bank, and that if they intended to carry their own baby then they were not in need of a surrogate. Having ruled out the first two couples, the last two were intriguing, and possible contenders, so I decided to meet up with them one at a time.

The first couple consisted of a young "B" list actress and her "Music Producer Husband". "The Young Actress" had been known as a sex symbol, and the husband had been fairly unknown until getting with "The Young Actress". They had wanted a second child but because of their scheduling (her with movies, him with recording artists) they were not able to carve out the time to make it happen. The concern was that the first child was getting older and they didn't want there to be too big an age difference between the two children. Their problem was common – wanting children but not wanting to slow down either of their careers – so I thought they might be a good fit.

They invited me to a home they were renting while "The Young Actress" was on location for a movie she was filming. As a general rule, they'd made it a point to travel together as much as possible. When I got there I was pleasantly surprised to meet a very non-Hollywood, normal type of family. They did not put on any airs and seemed very down to earth. Their current child was a total sweetheart and I liked this family immediately. We discussed the job, and surprisingly, they didn't make any crazy or unusual requests. They simply wanted to add to their family. The only concern was what they wanted to pay.

Whereas in the past I had always received at least half a million, they wanted to pay me only $250,000. That was not the kind of money that I was used to; I had always been paid at least double that. And not to sound uppity, I was used to being paid a lot more. As I sat in their backyard eating barbecued hamburgers that the "Music Producer Husband" had grilled, I found that I was still considering the job even though I would be paid drastically less. I tried to remember why I had got into this business in the first place, and it hadn't been for the money necessarily. Although the first time had been unplanned, the others had been to help others have children when they could not, for whatever reasons.

At one point "The Young Actress" asked if I wanted to take a swim in their pool, and when I told her that I had not packed a swimsuit, she told me I could use one of hers. I was excited to see that I could still look good in a two- piece, and that I could actually fit a bikini worn by a sex-symbol actress. When I came out in the two-piece, "The Young Actress" said "looking good" to me and the "Music Producer Husband" winked. While splashing around in the backyard pool with that all-American family, I made a decision that without even meeting the other couple I was going to be a surrogate for this couple. In fact, I decided that in spite of the pay cut it would be my honor to do something so nice for such a nice couple.

We decided that we would start in a month because "The Young Actress" had wanted to wait until she was done filming the movie she was currently filming, so that she could accompany me to my initial doctor's appointments. She would only be able to make the initial appointments because she was scheduled to start filming her next movie in six months. I agreed and we made plans to meet the following week when "The Young Actress" had a day off to sign the contracts and get the details hashed out.

About two days before the day we were scheduled to meet, the "Music Producer Husband" gave me a call and invited me out to his birthday celebration. I thought that was a super cool gesture and I readily accepted. I figured that there would be a lot of industry big-wigs at the party and I would get to rub elbows with some of them. At a minimum I thought I'd be able to hang out with the wife again, since she seemed so cool. I had assumed that she was able to get the day off to be there with her husband. I was wrong on both accounts.

There were no industry big-wigs at the party. "The Young Actress" was not even there. The only two people there were myself and the "Music Producer Husband". He had the area romantically lit, and when I looked around for his wife, he quickly "assured" me that she was at work and their child was with the nanny.

As if it wasn't obvious, I asked the "Music Producer Husband" what he was doing. And he told me that he was "making things more interesting." I wondered who, exactly, he was making things more interesting for. I respectfully declined his "offer" and he threw in a deal. He told me that if I let him impregnate me personally that he would throw in an additional 50 grand, making my total 300 grand. And he was serious.

Men! And their egos! I was so offended on so many levels that I didn't know where to start. But I let this egotistical, cheapskate, jerk have it. I told him that not only was 250 grand or even 300 grand a small amount of money, but that it was the least I'd been offered from any celebrity ever!

I saw that that stung his little ego, so I kept going. I told him that my womb was for sale, not me, and that he was a jerk for thinking he now had access to all of me simply because I was going to be a surrogate for him. I further insulted him by adding that 50 grand wouldn't purchase me, and now neither would 250 grand purchase my womb because I would never carry a child for him. I told him in no uncertain terms that the deal was off and that he and his wife would have to hire another surrogate.

Then, because he had put me in such an awkward situation, and because I would no longer get to work with what I thought was a great family, and because his wife and child deserved so much more than him, and because I just felt like it, I slapped his face as hard as I could and I left.

After my anger dissipated, I was confused on what to do. I didn't know if I should tell his wife what had happened or just extricate myself from this situation. One thing was for certain, and that is that I was not going to be working for this couple.

The next day, fearing what the husband would or would not tell his wife, I called "The Young Actress" and left a voicemail for her to call me when she got a chance.

It was the next day when she called me back. I told her that I'd received a better offer, and that I would not be able to sign on as their surrogate. I could hear the sadness in her voice. I knew she was disappointed in me, and I was angry that I let her think I was driven by money in making this decision.

I hated to "take the blame" for ending our professional relationship before it even began, but I didn't know how else to do it without causing tension in her home (that is, if she didn't already know that her husband was a scumbag).

The whole ordeal made me feel sad, and a bit dirty. I've thought about that situation many times since then and have concluded that it really was a shame that it came to that, because for all I knew the wife was a really good person and did not deserve what happened, but I knew I wouldn't have been able to work with that couple because the husband was a creep and I wouldn't have felt comfortable bringing a baby into that home.

I've struggled with not telling "The Young Actress" about what really happened, but since then I've obviously written this book. So, if the wife is now reading this, then she knows who she is. And she now knows – if she didn't already – that her husband is a creep. Oh well, on to the next couple...

Chapter 7: The Fourth Couple: Boys will be Boys

I was beginning to think my luck was running out, because I was meeting some really shady, questionable couples. It was becoming harder and harder to convince myself that I was doing this to help others. The type of people I was meeting and considering agreeing to work with were proof that my standards had become so low, and that I was obviously only in it for the money.

Maybe this was a sign that it was time for me to get out of this business. I was seriously thinking that my clock was ticking and my days as a celebrity surrogate were numbered.

For example, this current couple that I was considering working with were not as bad as the first couple – with the philandering husband trying to impregnate me personally - but they also had issues.

When the wife contacted me - a week after my ordeal with "The Young Actress" and her "Music Producer Husband" - at least she was honest in telling me that this baby was a last attempt to stay together. I don't know if she told me that because when I met them I would know who they were, and thus their "story" or if she was just being honest. But I had to admit that I respected the fact that she was upfront.

Honest or not though, I normally would have walked away from something like this, but the rest of what she told me gave me pause.

She said that they still loved each other but had some problems with infidelity in the past. They had been together since high school, before her husband, a famous sports player, had made it big. I can't say which sport because it would become obvious who I'm talking about, but "The Sports Player" and his wife had made a promise that they would not let the fame and fortune tear their bond.

As a young couple they had managed to make that promise last. But in the last few years, since her husband's star power had risen, it had become harder to keep the promise to each other.

She confided that her husband had gone from sneaking around cheating to openly cheating, and that although she wanted to stay with him, she wasn't sure if she could handle the disrespect. She said that although it was assumed that the wives of sports stars would put up with such infidelity, that she would not. She said she hoped that another child (they already had one) would solidify their bond and bring them closer together. She confessed that at a minimum she hoped that expanding their family would help her husband value what they had, grow up, and become a better man, husband, and father – especially if the second child was a boy.

She was so dead set on having a boy that she told me she wouldn't even consider the possibility that it could be a girl. She said she had prayed and God had revealed in a dream that it would be a boy and that the baby boy would save her family. I considered myself a believer in God, and did not doubt the merits of her dream, but I wanted to tell her that I had always heard that dreams meant the opposite. However, since I didn't want to crush her dream of giving her husband a mini version of himself, and thus a legacy, I kept my mouth quiet. I did, however, recommend the procedure that "Richie Rich" had used.

I told her there was a procedure that allowed the separation of x and y chromosomes so that a person could have the gender of child they wanted – male or female. She insisted that there was no need to do that because she already knew they would have a boy; her dream had told her so. She also said she did not want to do this procedure because she didn't want the word to get out that she was using a surrogate or that she had "manufactured a son."

So I did something that I don't normally do. I agreed to be a surrogate for a family that had questionable motives and didn't appear to be very solid, and I agreed to be their surrogate without meeting the husband in person.

I didn't know if it was because I felt sorry for the wife, or because I didn't have any more clients lined up at the moment, or because the husband had a legitimate reason for not being there (training camp), or because of the previous experience I'd had with the "Music Producer Husband" making me not want to meet another husband-client, but I did what I didn't normally do and made a decision based solely on my interaction with the wife. I would soon come to regret this decision.

It was agreed upon that we would start right away because the husband only had a short break in his training schedule, so we literally only had a day to receive the semen sample and make the implantation.

I wasn't expecting things to go as planned, partly because they never do, but also because we were rushing and not giving this process the amount of time it needed to work. Apparently the wife had had another dream about a baby growing in a flower (which she interpreted to mean my womb) and she was confident that it would happen right away.

Surprisingly she was right. Exactly four weeks later, with only that one try, it was confirmed that I was indeed pregnant. I thought to myself that maybe this wife was on to something as it pertained to this dream-to-get-answers business. In any case, I was pregnant and she was elated.

During the course of my first trimester, and indeed throughout the entire pregnancy, I became her pet project. She told me to sleep a certain way because it increased the likelihood of having a boy. She told me to eat certain foods, wear certain colors, and even pay attention to the direction in which the necklace around my neck swung, all in an effort to produce a boy.

When I hit the second trimester, and was about five months pregnant, at one of our doctor's visits (she accompanied me to them all) she was told that she could find out the sex. I was so anxious to know if it was a boy myself at that point. But I was surprised when she didn't accept the invitation to learn her baby's sex. She said to "peek" now would not be exercising faith that she was having a boy. I really respected and admired her faith and strong belief system, even if at times I was skeptical about it.

As the months went on, she treated me like I was her child. She sent me soup when I had the sniffles, and Sudoku puzzles to keep me mentally sharp. She lectured me on keeping physically active, and even requested that I say something positive about myself (out loud) and something positive to the baby (also out loud) every day. She was convinced that this practice would teach the baby the power of positivity.

I complied with her requests because, for one, they weren't harmful, and for two, because honestly, they were quite humorous and entertaining.

I can't tell you how many days I chuckled to myself as I said out loud to my stretch marks "I like you, as you are a part of me" or giggled as I said to the baby "You are a wonderful human being," all while knowing full well that it probably didn't even have ears yet, let alone an understanding of positivity.

In any case, I liked "The Sports Player's" wife a lot. I thought there was a lot more to her than just her pretty face and eccentricities. The only thing that truly annoyed me about her was how cheap, yet money-hungry she was. For example, she wanted us to eat at the best places, but she wanted everything discounted. And to ensure she got the best deals she had actually pulled out coupons as if everyone that saw her didn't know that she was a multimillionaire.

She reminded me of someone who didn't come from much money, and so tried hard to keep every cent of it that she could. I didn't remember much about my grandmother, since she had lived so far away from mom, dad, and died while I was fairly young; but I do remember that my grandmother used to call that a "poverty mentality." I was finally able to see what my grandmother meant. I just never thought I'd see a poverty mentality exist in a multimillionaire.

In any case, as I neared the seventh month of pregnancy, "The Sports Player's" wife let me know that she was pleased with the way I was carrying the baby.

Apparently I was carrying the baby heavy and low, like a basketball, which she took to mean I was having a boy.

She thanked me for doing what I needed to do to give them a boy. I told her that there was nothing I could do to give them a boy, that it all depended on her husband's sperm and she didn't seem to believe me. She said she believed the universe gave us whatever we wanted, we simply had to prepare ourselves to receive it.

She insisted that they were going to have a boy not just because she had dreamt it but because I had then followed all the necessary steps to make it happen.

I didn't bother arguing with her. I was tired and irritable, and was suffering from the worst heartburn that I'd ever experienced. I didn't know if it was just mental, and a sign that being pregnant all the time was getting old, but I was starting to have more and more pregnancy ailments, to the point where being pregnant was becoming annoying.

Over the course of the last few pregnancies, I had developed stretch marks, had morning and sometimes all-day sickness, and had skin reactions. For example, with this pregnancy I developed what's called a "pregnancy mask" over my face, which resembled a minor-looking case of psoriasis. It totally grossed me out. Plus, I was very short-tempered, and irritable. And to top it off, I couldn't stop crying.

When "The Sports Player's" wife witnessed my pregnancy difficulties, she responded by giving me a discounted coupon to a spa service. I was flabbergasted. This woman and her husband could afford to buy this spa, and yet all she had managed to do was give me a coupon for 35% off of a spa service, instead of paying for the service itself. Hello, I was carrying her child for crying out loud! Didn't I deserve more than just a coupon or discounted rate?

I comforted myself with daily affirmations that this pregnancy wouldn't last forever. And thankfully it didn't.

Although it seemed like the last two months of the pregnancy had moved at a snail's pace, eventually my due date came. And it went. Five days past my due date, the doctor decided to induce. He did this partly because I was overdue and also because "The Sports Player" had the next 72 hours off. In this way, the superstar and his wife could be there for the birth of their child.

I was induced and had the baby 15 hours later. This had been a difficult delivery. Not as bad as delivering "The Actress'" big baby, but this delivery was definitely long, drawn out, and painful, and once again I had to have an episiotomy.

I didn't know how much more of this my body could take. When I gave the final push – the one that pushed the baby out – I was so exhausted that I fell asleep before I could even see the parents' reaction to their little one or hear what the sex of the baby was.

That was the part of this process I loved the most, because no matter how rich, cold, eccentric, or entitled the celebrity was, when they met their baby for the first time, they were always so ecstatic and it was an opportunity to see them as their true self.

When the celebrity met their baby for the first time they were vulnerable, and I often got to catch a glimpse of who they were or might have been before they became famous.

When I came to, about an hour later, I was surprised to see sad faces all around me. My first instinct was to wonder what had happened to the baby. I was terrified that something bad had happened.

Even though these were not my biological children that I carried, I still felt a bond with them because they had been inside me for so long. I sat up quickly and shrieked, "Where's the baby?!" I was met with a dry response of, "It's in the nursery," from "The Sports Player's" wife.

I looked around to see why there were sad faces, and as if in an answer to my unspoken question, "The Sports Player's wife" commented that the baby was a girl. She said that so sadly that one would've thought she was saying that the baby had passed away.

I looked over at "The Sport's Player", who despite just delivering his baby I had only met twice, and in his defense he looked apologetic. Still, he comforted his wife by stroking her back as if they had just received some bad news.

I was amazed. Even the nurse that entered the room seemed crestfallen, like she too had gotten the memo that a tragedy had just occurred.

Apparently, the whole time I was out, "The Sports Player's" wife had never even held the baby, and although I think "The Sports Player" would've liked to hold the baby girl, he looked as if he dared not, lest he upset his wife.

I was ashamed of the way they were acting, and sad for this baby I had never even seen, so I did something I didn't normally do. I asked the couple if they minded if I held the baby. The wife replied that she didn't care what I did with her. And with tears in my eyes, I held what I thought was the most beautiful baby girl I had ever seen.

The baby girl looked at me with eyes that were so clear, and with such a steady gaze – especially for a newborn – that I knew she was going to be someone special. I held that baby and rocked her to me and my heart broke for her as I watched her biological parents stare at her with what can best be described as animosity. There was not a single feeling of love anywhere in that room, and I found myself wondering if I should adopt her and take her away from these ungrateful fools.

I didn't have long to wonder about that possibility, because eventually "The Sports Player's" wife asked to hold the baby, and I think that was only because she was growing jealous that someone else was holding her baby. She held the baby and just stared at her, as if seeking confirmation that the baby was indeed a girl. After holding the baby girl for a little while, and allowing her husband to hold the baby for about five minutes, they left the hospital.

That was a first! Since becoming a celebrity surrogate, I had never had the biological parents leave the hospital after their baby was born! I sat there – or more like laid there - uncertain of what to do. The only thing I knew for sure was that I had to hold that baby. While I had the chance, I planned to try to infuse so much love into that baby, because I wasn't so sure she would get it at home. In my heart I hoped that things would change and that the wife would come to her senses and realize that she had a beautiful baby regardless of her sex.

That whole day – especially since it became apparent that "The Sports Player" and his wife were not returning to the hospital – I just held that baby and rocked her and gave her all the love I could give.

The next day when "The Sports Player's" wife showed up bright and early, I took that as a sign that she was ready to give this another shot. I figured that she must've felt bad about the way she acted towards her own daughter and was coming back to the hospital bright and early because she had slept fitfully and probably couldn't wait to get back there.

I was stunned when she walked into the room and without asking to hold the baby (who was lying in my arms) declared that she was not paying for my services since she did not get what she'd wanted.

I didn't think I'd heard her right. So very calmly I asked her to repeat herself. She stated, very clearly, as if talking to a child, that she was not going to pay the one million dollars we had agreed upon because I had not held up my end of the bargain.

Normally, I received half of the money at the beginning of the second trimester and the final half of the money on my due date. It was done that way because the second trimester usually marked a period where the risk of miscarriage was greatly minimized and so it was assumed that the pregnancy was viable.

The final half was paid on the due date so that by the time the baby came, the final payment would have been made, and the celebrity wouldn't have had to take focus away from their new baby, whom they'd be so anxious to meet.

Since they had already paid me the first payment, "The Sports Player's" wife was threatening to withhold the second half of their payment. While there in the hospital, I had to call my attorney who had helped me draw up the NDA and contract papers - and who I still have to this day – to have them prepare the legal documents necessary to file suit. When my attorney made contact with "The Sports Player's" attorney, and they saw that I was serious about pursuing this matter legally instead of just letting it slide, they quickly changed their tune and made my final payment.

I didn't know if they thought I was doing something illegal and didn't have legal recourse, or if they had thought that I would fear exposure and would simply forgive the "debt," but they were sadly mistaken. If I didn't know anything else I knew that I was at least familiar enough with the law to understand what was right versus wrong. I knew that contracts were legally binding and considering that I had wanted to be an attorney at one point, I was fully willing to fight it out in court.

After the payment was made, "The Sports Player's" wife had a nanny come and immediately pick up the baby. It pained me that she would not do it herself, and it pained me even more to think that this baby might not get the love she deserved simply because she wasn't a boy.

In the months following, I saw news stories of this couple and their new "bundle of joy" in which "The

Sports Player's" wife seemed to dote on the child and appear to be the loving mother.

I hoped and prayed that those displays of affection were real and not contrived for the camera. At that point all I could do was hope and pray. Because of how nasty this situation got, I decided to take a long break away from being a celebrity surrogate to rejuvenate my mind and body. I even considered not returning at all.

Either way, I knew I needed to get away from this career that suddenly seemed to do more harm than good.

Chapter 8: The Fifth and Final Couple: Enough is Enough!

I made plans to take a year off. After the stress of having carried so many babies for so many celebrities, I felt I needed a break. I wasn't even sure if I was going to go back to doing it again. Maybe it was just me, but I felt like each couple had become more and more demanding, and I was becoming less and less excited about what I was doing. For lack of a better word I had begun to feel *used*, whereas before that I had at least felt like I was helping people – and getting paid in the process.

I spent the first month of my year off just resting. Pregnancy takes a lot of energy, and no matter how much sleep I got, I always felt like I needed more. I spent my mornings sleeping. I would wake up around noon and have some lunch. Go back to bed, and then wake up in time for dinner. And then I'd sleep some more. I didn't know how pregnant women who had kept their children managed. Those women had given birth, brought the baby home, and then had to wake up all times of night to care for the child. I couldn't imagine having to do that. I mean, when did they rest?

About three weeks into my first month off, I was finally starting to feel like my old self again. The thing is, I did not look like my old self. All of my previous pregnancies had taken a toll on my body.

My skin looked tired and so did my eyes. My teeth weren't as white because I had not been able to keep up with my bleaching treatments, and my hair was thick, long, and beautiful because of all of the prenatal vitamins, but it was unkempt and had faded back to its normal dull color.

My breasts were still bigger than they had been before the pregnancies, but now they had a little bit of a droop to them. If someone says that after pregnancy your breasts don't begin to sag a bit, they're lying. Unless of course your boobs are too small to sag, then that's another story.

My hips were wider, which again suited my femininity. But I was just overall a bit out of shape - both mind and body. To restore myself, I did something that I'd never done before. I resorted to yoga.

Because I now had so much money, and I didn't want to do something as personal as yoga in front of a lot of other people, I hired a personal yoga instructor. My first session of yoga was spent thinking about all the things I had to do. For example, I made to-do lists and put in such items as: getting my hair done, getting a fresh mani-pedi, getting professionally refitted for my proper bra size (I think I was now a certified DD cup), and I had even thought of what I would like to do with myself moving forward.

I knew that I could not be a surrogate forever, and even if I could I knew that I would not want to. I thought about going back to school and becoming that lawyer my parents had always wanted me to be. But I knew I wasn't cut out for school. I had already seen and done too much to be restricted to a classroom setting. I wanted to explore life, and actually live life, instead of just preparing to.

I thought of jumping back into the club promotion business. Because of the time I spent being a celebrity surrogate, I had made a ton of contacts, and I knew I could parlay those into making my business successful. But the thought of entering the club promotion business again made me tired.

Truthfully, I did not want to do anything that would take a lot of effort. I wanted the opportunity to live life to the fullest. I wanted to travel and shop, to wine and dine, and if I was being very honest with myself, I will admit that I also wanted to fall in love.

I wanted to meet a man that could make me laugh, someone who wasn't pretentious and cocky. I wanted to meet a man who had a big family so that I could belong. I wanted to get married in a small, intimate ceremony (because the more I hung around celebrities the less I liked flashiness and showboating). Then, I wanted children.

I had grown tired of carrying babies and handing them over. I liked to think that I did not feel attached to the children that I carried, and outwardly I appeared like I was not. But somewhere on the inside I felt like each and every one of the babies I carried had a special piece of my heart, and maybe even a small piece of my soul. I wanted to share my heart and soul with my own little one. I wanted to go through my own pregnancy and carry my own baby. I wanted to name a baby, to love it, to dress it, to hold it, to talk to it as it grew in my belly and let it know that I was its mom.

I didn't know where all this was coming from. But I knew that it was how I was really feeling on the inside, and that my days of being a celebrity surrogate were coming to an end.

Needless to say, with all that on my mind, my first attempt at yoga was anything but peaceful. But I had dedicated the second month of my "break" to learning and perfecting yoga. I figured yoga would help me regain my peace of mind as well as some of my muscle tone.

The next day when the yoga instructor came, I confided in him that I was having a hard time slowing my mind down long enough to concentrate on the yoga poses. He took it even slower, played some calming music that resembled rain falling from the sky, and without me even realizing it, I was able to spend the full hour feeling very tranquil.

As the days went on, I got better and better at yoga. I had purchased the "raindrops" CD that my yoga instructor played that second day, and I would listen to it while I cleaned or read a book or just relaxed in my apartment.

I hated cleaning, and could definitely afford to hire a housekeeper, but the experience I had with "The Actress" and her housekeeper/spy left me fearful of ever having a housekeeper again. Somehow listening to my meditation CD actually helped me enjoy cleaning.

I spent month number three in Paris. I had wanted the opportunity to explore a different culture, to get away from the loftiness and self-centeredness of L.A.

While in Paris I booked the penthouse suite of a luxurious hotel and did all the things that I previously would've only been able to dream about. I drank wine and ate cheese in the morning, I went to many museums and historical landmarks, and I shopped until I had filled up the penthouse.

I shopped so much that I had to mail many of my items home before I even left Paris. I got a French tutor, and began my journey of learning French. I somehow knew that my learning French would make mom and dad proud.

I had so much fun in Paris that I decided to extend my travels. I decided to also spend the next month abroad. The first two weeks I spent in Spain, and the second half of the month I spent in Italy.

This was probably the best time of my life. Being in Paris, Spain and Italy reawakened the creative side of me. I began to remember when as a child I became interested in painting, and poetry.

While out browsing the shops and bistros, I picked up a journal and began to write. I wrote about my experiences, I wrote about the people I'd met, and I reflected on what I would like to see for my future.

I figured that I wanted to do something that would allow me to travel when and where I wanted, something that would allow me to have a family and the freedom and flexibility to be with them, something that would allow me to make a lot of money, and something that would make mom and dad proud.

Throughout my travels I kept playing those criteria over and over in my head, wondering what type of job would allow me to do the things I wanted. I figured that I could always just live on the money I had already made, but I had seen what happened with restless, rich celebrities. I wanted to do something with my life other than shop, party, and experiment with drugs, like some restless, rich celebrities did.

One day I was in Italy sitting down and enjoying a cappuccino and delle uova, il Pane con della marmellata e del burro (eggs, with bread and jam), when it suddenly came to me. I decided that I would become a writer.

Writing would give me the opportunity to express myself creatively without putting any limitations on me. For example, I could write anywhere in the world and about anything I chose.

I decided that I would begin by writing about my experiences as a celebrity surrogate. I never planned to publish this. Initially it was just a way to begin writing - I had only chose to write on this topic because it was the subject that I knew the most about because of my previous experiences.

I went back to the beginning of my journey and I wrote about my life growing up with my parents. I wrote about classmates I had known, teachers that had influenced me, my awkward high school years, my dramatic college experiences.

I wrote about my parents' death, and for the first time I really started to deal with my feelings about that. I wrote about that dark time in my life after they died, and how I'd been a young woman simply trying to find myself.

I wrote about Sammi, and how she'd been a bright light in an otherwise dark existence. I wrote about my relationship with Eddie, my relationship with "Shades", and how all of these life events had lined up and culminated in my becoming a celebrity surrogate.

I wrote about the abortion I had. I wrote about the baby I had with "Shades" and how it had felt to give her up. I wrote about all the babies I had carried. I wrote about all the couples I had met, the ones I had worked with and the ones I had turned away. I wrote about all their little quirks, their secrets and lies, their vulnerabilities.

Through my writing, for the first time, I was able to see many of them as regular human beings. Sure, they had a lot of money and power, but they were just as flawed as the rest of us. They just went to more extremes to hide it. And I wrote about those extremes too.

I just let it all hang out. And because the information was so potentially scandalous, I was very careful about not putting in identifying information. It was almost like without even realizing it, I was already preparing myself to make this a book.

I didn't put in any names because God forbid I lost the journal, I wouldn't want someone to find it. This information in the wrong hands could be used in a very bad way. I knew that most of my couples would probably pay any amount of money to not have these stories told, so I made sure to protect them with my life.

All of that writing left me feeling refreshed. I hadn't realized that I had gone through so much, that I was being held captive by so much emotional baggage. Writing all of it down had a way of releasing me from it. I felt happy and whole in a way I had never felt before, not even when mom and dad were alive. This confirmed for me that I was meant to be a writer. I finally felt that I had found my calling.

During the fifth month of my self-imposed break, I returned back to the States. I felt so renewed and so refreshed. I had gotten to a point where I wrote wherever I was.

I wrote first thing in the morning when I woke up. I wrote after breakfast. I wrote before lunch. I wrote after lunch. I wrote about everything from cookbooks I liked to write, based on mom's recipes, to a book about dealing with abortion, to fiction novels about love and marriage. I even wrote a short fictional story loosely based around me and Sammi.

I spent the next seven months writing because I loved it, and running because numerous pregnancies had readjusted my body fat composition to a point where I now had to work out a little bit if wanted to keep my figure.

After taking a year off, to write and get my body back in order, I was ready to go. I figured I would be a celebrity surrogate a few more times as I wrote my books. And when I had enough books to publish, I would stop being a surrogate.

On a Monday evening I put myself back in business. I can't discuss what that entails, because it might give me and my clients away, but not even an hour later I had been contacted.

The e-mail was vague, but the details were clear. In the e-mail I was to meet someone at a certain location at a certain time wearing a certain color so that I could be identified. For security reasons I never posted a picture of myself, but I always made sure to give my description and my dimensions. The person on the other end of the e-mail informed me that they were prepared to confirm that my description and dimensions were accurate.

The e-mail was worded in a very no-nonsense way, which didn't bother me, except that it had me very curious about who could be on the other end. I replied, attached my contracts and the necessary information, and resent the e-mail. The meeting had been arranged.

Over the next couple weeks as I awaited my meeting with "The Anonymous Person", I scheduled a couple other meetings. The meeting with "The Anonymous Person" was sandwiched between two other meetings – one meeting before theirs and one meeting after. At the first scheduled meeting I met a "Country Singer" and her husband. They seemed very nice and very normal, and my instinct was to go with them. They offered 1.5 million, and when I told them that my going rate was 2 million, they agreed to pay it right away.

They did not try to haggle me as celebrities were often famous for doing.

Over the years of working with celebrities, I had come to know that although they were often very rich, they were also very stingy and cheap. They liked to either get things for free or deeply discounted. But mostly they liked to get it free.

This couple readily agreed to the 2 million and seemed just as eager to work with me as I was to work with them. However, I was very honest in telling them that I had two more meetings set up, and that I would not be able to confirm our arrangement until after I had met with the other two potential clients. They said they understood that. We shook hands, finished lunch, and all in all had a very pleasant afternoon together. In hindsight I realize that if I had gone with that couple, this story might have never been told, let alone published.

Later in the week I met with "The Anonymous Person" that had sent that very vague e-mail. The location where they chose for us to meet was very far away from any celebrity hotspots. It was in a nondescript location where one would not expect to meet very many people. Right away I knew I would be meeting with a very big celebrity, and I began to imagine who it might be.

Twenty minutes later when a very curious-looking person walked through the door, I was astonished to see that it was not a big celebrity at all. As a matter of fact I didn't recognize the person at all. Since I had always been pretty up on the who's who of celebrities, I assumed that this person was not in show business, and was what was considered "a quiet millionaire."

The person walked over to me with a notebook and a pen ready to do business. We introduced ourselves, and very quickly I learned that this person was a representative of "The Anonymous Person". Without apology this person explained to me that they were there on behalf of "The Anonymous Person" to assess and confirm my dimensions (complete with taking my measurements via measuring tape) and confirm my description (multi-ethnic, plain-looking with no exotic features, pretty).

After my assessment and appraisal, this person then handed me a series of contracts with everything from NDAs to failure-to-appear clauses. There were no less than eight contracts ranging from 25 to 50 pages each.

I'd only skimmed over them because the representative assured me that I would get to take them home and read them more thoroughly with my attorney if I chose to. But in scanning the contracts I was able to ascertain that I would need to sign off that I wouldn't talk about anything explicitly, that I wouldn't go anywhere that the client specifically restricted, that I would act in the manner of an employee, that I would agree to eat or not eat what they told me, be under strict medical care of their choosing, wear or not wear what they told me, hold them faultless in any regard including if this pregnancy caused my death, and not make any future contact with them including attendance at any of their concerts. That last line was my first indication that I was dealing with a major recording artist.

In addition to the contracts and the assessment and appraisal of my physical features, the representative of "The Anonymous Person" wanted me to take an IQ test and a test of emotional stability.

I had seen some audacious things in my day, and in the business that I was in, not very much surprised me. But I must admit that I was surprised by this request. Since I would be using their eggs and sperm, I wondered what my IQ had to do with anything. At the end of the day, I was just the oven baking their bun. I told the representative as much. Then I became very indignant as I explained to the representative that I had many clients who were awaiting my service and that I did not have to take the disrespectful requests of this person.

I said all this while standing up preparing to leave the table and end all dealings with whoever this "Anonymous Person" was. The representative, who I later found out was one of their attorneys, slid a piece of paper across the table to me. The representative then quietly said to me, "Please look at the total offer before you make up your mind." I halfheartedly reached across the table, grabbed the piece of paper from the representative and flipped it open. Written on the piece of paper was the number 5,000,000. I just looked at it and blinked. I was so dumbfounded that I initially did not know what the 5 million was supposed to represent.

When the representative/attorney informed me that the 5 million was the amount that I was to be paid, needless to say, I sat back down. For $5 million I would not only take the IQ test they proposed, I would've probably also done a military style boot camp drill to show my athleticism. $5 million has a way of humbling even the haughtiest person. And despite what I figured was a ridiculous request, I was immediately humbled. At that point I was willing to do whatever - to an extent – "The Anonymous Person" wanted me to do.

The $5 million I would make from this job would be equivalent to taking two and a half other jobs. It's as if the $5 million I was making to be this couple's celebrity surrogate was equivalent to being pregnant for twenty two and a half months. Specifically, for nine months of pregnancy I would be paid as if I had performed twenty two and half months of pregnancy. I figured if I could get a few more contracts like this, I could surely retire from surrogacy and fully embrace my writing. The truth is, with that amount I could have retired then. But I knew the extra money would set me up nicely, especially since I didn't know how long it would take me to "hit it big" as a bestselling author.

Over the next couple weeks I fulfilled the requirements. I had taken the IQ test, an emotional IQ test, a urinalysis, and had signed all the contracts. I did all this without even meeting "The Anonymous Person".

After I had completed all the information to "The Anonymous Person's" satisfaction, another face-to-face meeting was arranged. I thought I'd finally get to see who this person was.

We picked a date and a time and agreed to meet right outside of New York. This was the first time I would meet a client in this particular area, but since they sent me the plane ticket and everything had been legitimate so far, I didn't see why this would be a problem.

The location was to be a nondescript hotel suite. It was not the actual room that I was staying in, nor was it near to the hotel where I was staying. They actually put me up in a really nice luxury hotel, but the place where we were to meet was anything but. It might've been luxury according to non-celebrity people's standards, but I could tell without even having met this couple that they were a really big deal.

When I got to the designated meeting spot, I checked into the hotel room, sat on the sofa and watched a little bit of television. I must've fallen asleep, because when someone started opening the door, I was startled awake.

I looked over at the clock and realized I had been asleep for two hours, which meant that "The Anonymous Person" was two hours late. I got the feeling that this couple was used to making people wait for them.

I sat up on the sofa, turned off the television and waited to see who it was. The anticipation was killing me. When the person turned the corner and we met for the first time face-to-face I was in awe.

This was not the actual "Anonymous Person", but it was someone just as recognizable - it was her mom! This person's mom had been in the media just as much as "The Anonymous Person", and when I saw the mom, and then put two and two together and realized who the client was, I felt like a little child. I was so nervous and just downright shell-shocked that it took me a moment to even speak.

"The Anonymous Person's" mom came into the room accompanied by two big bulky guys, who I assumed were bodyguards. "The Anonymous Person's" mom asked me if she could sit. I nodded my head yes because I literally could not find the words.

As she sat next to me saying nothing, and I sat next to her in a cold sweat, the two bodyguards went around the room looking for something. They looked in drawers, they looked between the sheets, under the bed, in corners and closets, and they opened and closed all of the doors.

145

Because everything seemed like it was moving in slow motion, and because I was so shocked to be working with who I was going to be working with, it took me a minute to realize that the security team was probably looking for bugs. They were probably looking to see if I was recording this meeting. These people were not playing around! They meant business!

I had already signed the forms authorizing them to do a background investigation on me because I had nothing to hide, and I knew that with the kind of money these people had, they would be able to find out about every nook and cranny of my life (even without the written authorization).

Like I said, I had nothing to hide and no dirty secrets - aside from the fact that I was a secret celebrity surrogate - so I authorized the peek into my life (more like rummage), and I sat amused as I watched the security team tear up the hotel room looking for any kind of trap.

When they were satisfied that I was not recording the meeting or trying to film it, the security team exited the room and as I was left there face-to-face with the most famous mom in the world. It briefly occurred to me that she might actually be the one hiring me to be a surrogate for her, but considering the fact that she was already a grandmother and her famous children were already grown, I seriously doubted that she was the client.

After a brief pause, in which it seemed we were both assessing each other, she spoke. She said, "You know who I am?" It was meant to be a question, I think, but it actually came off more like an assertion. I dumbly nodded yes because I still could not find the words. She then said, "So I guess you also know who is interested in hiring you?" I again nodded yes. She looked at me quizzically. So I finally spoke up and stuttered, "Yes. Yes, ma'am." She smiled at that. Though it wasn't a "My, what a nice young lady you are kind of smile." It seemed a bit more calculated and menacing.

The whole time I sat talking to this beautiful and regal woman, I was intimated beyond words. Before her children became so famous this mom had initially been in the beauty industry, but I thought she would've made a wonderful interrogator, because talking to her made me feel like I was interviewing for a position with the CIA. She miraculously managed to convey warmth, and a cold standoffishness, all at the same time. I alternated between wanting to cuddle up to her and tell her all my secrets, and wanting to stand ten feet away from her so that she couldn't read my soul. I always thought she had been in the background of her children's careers, but after meeting with her, I'd be willing to bet that she controlled much of their success. She questioned me about everything from my political views, my education, people I'd met, the way I'd grown up, and plans I had for my future.

Even though I had traveled the world at that point, and had made quite a lot of money for myself, I felt like a panic-stricken little child sitting next to her. I answered all of her questions, many times with my eyes downcast, because I was just that intimidated.

Finally when the interview was over, she walked over to the front door of the hotel room and slightly knocked on it. In walked the two big burly bodyguards. As they stood there dutifully beside her, she walked back over to me, shook my hand and said it was nice to meet me, and just like that she was gone.

I felt mentally and physically exhausted. I felt like I'd had a fight and a hard test all at the same time. I mean, I was so exhausted I literally lay across the bed and took a nap. When I awoke, about 45 minutes later, I grabbed my things and exited the hotel room. As I left the room and took the elevator down I was constantly looking around for some sign that I had met with "The Anonymous Person's" mom. I think I was trying to reassure myself that I had not dreamt the entire encounter. That it had actually happened.

When I got to the front desk, I turned in the room key and proceeded to walk out of the hotel and over to the valet station. When I got to the valet station I heard someone behind me yell, "Ma'am, wait, stop!" I came to a stop and turned around just in time to be handed an envelope from the front desk clerk. My car was pulled around at the same time, so I didn't open the envelope until I got home.

When I got home and opened the envelope, I saw that it had come from "The Anonymous Person's" mom. In the letter were two lines that would change my life forever. The lines were: "You're hired. Expect a call with more details sometime today."

I fell back on the sofa with the letter clutched tightly to me. I wasn't sure if I was happy or sad. And I wasn't even sure why I was having such conflicting emotions. On the one hand I knew that I would be paid a large sum of money, and that I was on my way to being out of this career for good. On the other hand I somehow, intrinsically, felt that I was entering a different league, that this experience would be more than what I had bargained for.

Yet I knew I would not be able to turn away from the money. So on that day I made up my mind to become a celebrity surrogate for one of the world's most famous couples.

"The Anonymous Person's" mom was right. Sometime later that day I did receive a phone call. During the phone call I was told that I would be picked up from my apartment and driven to meet "The Anonymous Person" in person.

I asked the caller if they needed my address and he told me that they already had it. I thought to myself, *See, I knew that they had me investigated!* Sure enough, on the designated day, I received a call from my doorman letting me know that my driver had arrived. I got into the car and was driven to a private airport.

I somehow thought that we'd be meeting at a hotel or restaurant, but given the caliber of celebrity this person was, I guess I wasn't surprised that we would be meeting in a more discreet location. I wondered where they were flying me to. Briefly – and maybe because I watched too many movies - it occurred to me that they could kill me and no one would ever know, except maybe my doorman. I chuckled at that. I reassured myself that they wouldn't kill me when they obviously needed me to do a job for them. A very important job at that.

I was ushered into the private plane and seated comfortably. This was the most beautiful, most opulent airplane I had ever seen before, even in magazines. Everything was gold and marble, and the seats were butterscotch yellow with the softest leather material I had ever felt before in my life.

I sat down in what I imagine a cloud might feel like. I was offered refreshments and hors d'oeuvres. When I declined them, the person offering them exited the plane and I was left alone.

I took in my surroundings, and for a moment closed my eyes and imagined that all this was mine. When I heard the door to the private plane open, I assumed it was the pilot. What I saw instead nearly made me wet my designer pants. In walked "The Anonymous Person" and her husband! I could not believe I was in the same space as two of the most famous people in the world.

They walked in surrounded by security. After a check of the surroundings, the security left and the husband sat down without acknowledging me. He gave me a brief once over but sat away from me in a position that allowed him to keep an uninterested eye on me.

"The Anonymous Person" walked up to me and shook my hand. She was the most beautiful person I'd ever seen. She was even more beautiful in person, if that was even possible. Her skin appeared so golden and shiny that I was tempted to touch it. She radiated luxury and style. She had her hair pulled back in a ponytail and her eyes were like liquid gold. She was surprisingly tall, but that can be attributed to the fact that she was wearing six or seven inch heels.

As she shook my hand she gave me the most beautiful smile. I think I was instantly wrapped around her finger. Although this was probably one of the most famous people in the world, she seemed so down to earth, even though she looked and smelled and resembled a goddess.

She sat down and formally introduced herself and her husband, even though I obviously knew who they were.

I found the gesture very endearing. I was surprised to see that she seemed almost timid and shy. This person who had sold out hundreds or thousands of arenas seemed so normal and laid-back, and accommodating.

I had to remind myself that this was a business transaction, because the way she was treating me made me feel as if she and I were old friends. I couldn't get over the fact that she seemed so normal, despite being drop dead gorgeous. As a matter of fact, she seemed to be as nervous as I was, which made me feel even more endeared to her.

She asked me if I was hungry or thirsty. I was thirsty, but I didn't dare tell her that. I didn't want to move or speak too much. I found myself afraid that I might pass out in her presence.

She took it all in stride and ordered herself and me a glass of water. She asked her husband if he wanted anything and he shook his head no. He then put on a pair of headphones, put his feet up, and prepared to take a nap.

The word I would use to describe her legendary husband was *uninterested*. He seemed completely uninterested by the whole thing, as if he had other things to do. Or rather, better things to do. Without her saying a word, I instantly knew that she was running this particular show. And that having a child had been her idea.

As the plane took off, she confided in me that although she had flown "a million times or more" she was still very nervous flying. She then bowed her head, I assumed to say a little prayer. When she was done, off we flew. I still didn't know where we were going. And neither did I care. I was so excited to be sitting next to this person. It felt like I had won some sort of contest and not like I was being hired to do a job -specifically the job of carrying her child.

Initially we made small talk. She asked me about where I grew up, and whether or not I had brothers and sisters, the type of questions I knew she already had the answer to. But I appreciated that she was trying to break the ice. Although I would've loved to, I didn't dare ask her any questions. I didn't know if I was allowed to.

After a few minutes of small talk, the questions became a bit more personal. She asked me what made me become a celebrity surrogate. I confided in her that it was not something I had planned on doing. I told her how I had become unexpectedly pregnant and had chosen to give the baby to its father because he was in a more stable relationship. She seemed to sit with that information for a minute, almost as if she was trying to process it and see how she felt about it.

She then asked me how many babies I had carried and how I felt about giving them up. I told her how many there had been and I told her that I never felt anything about giving them up because I'd never really felt like they were mine to begin with. She nodded her head very vigorously at that answer, as if it was the right answer, the answer she had been waiting for.

She asked me if I was seeing anyone, and I told her no. She asked me about my family and friends, and I told her that I was pretty much alone. That I lost my parents and that of the two good friends I'd had, one had gotten married and moved on with her life, and the other one and I had simply grown apart. I didn't dare tell her that the latter one had been the wife of the man who had fathered my child, and that they had become the recipient of my first "surrogate" child. For some reason I held back that information.

She asked if I ever wanted a family of my own one day. And I told her a half-truth. I told her that I did one day (the truth), but that I didn't want to settle down and have children anytime soon because I was so young and still had a lot more that I wanted to accomplish before that happened (not quite true).

The truth is that I did want my own family and children sometime soon, but I did not want to scare her off and make her think that I might try to keep her child. So I kept that bit of information to myself.

She seemed to be satisfied with all my answers. We talked some more, and our conversation covered everything from celebrity gossip and chit-chat to what was going on in the news. To say she was such a superstar, I found her very well informed. I don't know why this surprised me. Maybe because with all the money she had she could've easily paid someone to do her reading for her. Nevertheless, the whole encounter with her was pleasantly surprising, and I was beginning to think that foreboding feeling I'd initially had from her mom was my own imagination.

After a few hours in the sky we landed. When the doors opened "The Anonymous Person" told me that it had been nice to meet me, but she stayed seated. I took that as a cue that I was to leave. I wanted to ask where they were dropping me off at, but I was still too afraid to say too many words to her. My mind was racing. I wondered where I was. I wondered where they had brought me to. And why weren't they also getting off the plane?

As I stepped off the plane into the bright sunlight, it took me a minute to realize that I was back where we'd started. We hadn't actually flown anywhere. In hindsight, I thought that was actually quite clever to have our meeting in the sky. That way, no one could trace us, and there weren't any paparazzi around to trail and document our meeting. I suddenly realized these people were a lot smarter (and more careful) than I'd given them credit for.

After I de-boarded their private plane they took off to God only knows where, and I went back home, already anticipating the next time I would get to meet that megastar.

I waited every day for a call or message from "The Anonymous Person". None ever came. I wondered if they were still interested in working with me. I wondered if I'd said or did something that had turned "The Anonymous Person" and/or her "Uninterested Husband" off.

After not hearing from them for over a week, I reasoned that they'd probably found someone more beautiful, more stylish, more intelligent than I to work with. With the amount of money they had at their disposal, I knew that they had many options if they were in the market for a celebrity surrogate.

Although celebrity surrogacy is not often talked about, it does exist, and there are many more celebrity surrogates out there. Celebrity surrogacy is an illustrious career shrouded in secrecy. So I knew that if they'd decided to find a different surrogate, it wasn't like they would have called me to tell me. I just figured that in due time I would probably hear the announcement that "The Anonymous Person is expecting!" Then I'd know that someone out there had been hired to do the job.

Or maybe there was no job to do. Maybe "The Anonymous Person" wasn't interested in having a baby at all, or if she was, maybe she intended to carry her own baby. For all I knew our meeting could've been about her researching a movie role. But then I thought, *Why would she have had me fill out so much information?*

Whatever the case, while on my morning run, I had decided that I would also move on and either call the initial couple I met with, or schedule a meeting with the other couple that had expressed an interest.

I got home, took a shower, and sat at my computer desk with my morning café au lait looking up the contact information for the first couple I'd met with. I had decided I would work with them instead of calling the other couple.

I located the information and just as I was preparing to call them, my phone rang. I answered it and to my surprise, it was "The Anonymous Person" herself. She had called personally to let me know that they had decided to hire me to carry their baby. I was ecstatic, although I remained calm and professional.

I was ecstatic for a couple reasons. Of course I was excited about the money. After all, this was going to be my largest payout yet. But I was also genuinely excited to work with such a huge megastar who seemed so cool and down to earth, despite her scary mom and uninterested husband.

As with the vast majority of my clients, she informed me that we would need to get started right away. I assumed it was because she had some projects coming up that she did not want to be "pregnant" for. I already knew that she had planned to pretend to be pregnant during the pregnancy because of the paperwork and contracts I had to sign.

The contracts spoke of complete and utter confidentiality, of me being out of the public eye, of never mentioning her or that a pregnancy existed, or in her case didn't exist, etcetera.

Her contract had been very specific (as contracts tend to be) and very stringent. The contract provided that I was going to be sequestered and not allowed any visitors. I also would have to get a complete physical and medical work over.

It was also made very clear that our contract would be contingent upon me following all directives, especially as it pertained to health and confidentiality. Health concerned eating what they told me, exercising as deemed appropriate, doctor's visits, and basically staying healthy; and confidentiality entailed never saying a word about this to anyone at any time, even one hundred years into the future. Believe it or not, the contract actually said that!

I had signed on the dotted line, with the intention to never say a word, after all, who would I tell? Little did I know how things would change.

When all the legalities were out of the way and I had signed her contracts, and of course met all her requirements, and she had signed mine as well, she informed me that we would need to start right away. I told her that I usually took folic acid before the procedure. She told me not to worry about that, that her personal doctor would give me everything that I needed and personally attend to this pregnancy.

The in vitro fertilization procedure was scheduled for one week from the day she called. After the procedure was confirmed successful, I was to fly to a quiet, remote location where I would stay for the entire pregnancy. I would be attended by "The Anonymous Person's" personal medical team, which consisted of a live-in Obstetrician, his registered nurse, and a registered dietician. My diet would consist of purely organic healthy meals, such as whole grains, fruits and veggies, lean meats, and nonfat dairy. Fats, sweets and anything not on the list were strictly forbidden and simply wouldn't be served by the live-in chef. On this private island were the people I'd already listed as well as a housekeeper and a grounds keeper, and a security team.

Of all the people there, the only person who knew that I was carrying a baby for this couple was the Obstetrician, and the only reason he knew was because he was going to personally deliver the baby, though not on the island. They didn't tell me much about where the baby would be delivered – I knew it would either be her hometown or where she currently resided – but they did tell me that it would be in a hospital.

I would later learn that they were having a private wing actually built in the hospital to further ensure complete anonymity and confidentiality.

Other than the doctor, the other staff members just thought that I was an extremely wealthy young woman that wanted to enjoy my pregnancy in private and away from the public eye as so many celebrities do. They never met "The Anonymous Person". I was flown to the island alone and the team was already assembled there when I got there. They too had signed confidentiality agreements and contracts committing to staying on the island for the duration of my pregnancy.

Before the implantation, I had my physical from the same doctor that would accompany me to the island. When I received my clean bill of health, I began to pack for the trip. I was only allowed to bring a few items and those were inspected. I was allowed to bring a photo of my deceased parents, a couple novels, my Ipod, and a few toiletries. Everything else, I was told, would be provided for me.

I was only allowed to communicate directly with the Obstetrician and I was also given a military style phone that only called "The Anonymous Person" and was only able to receive calls from "The Anonymous Person". I was not allowed to bring a journal (I guess to prevent me from documenting the experience), so I was not able to write many of the details. That was fine because the NDA and confidentiality agreements would've prevented me from disclosing many of the details anyway.

What follows from here is a remembered account of what transpired during my pregnancy for "The Anonymous Person".

I remember we started IVF on a Monday. I remember this because as most normal people were starting their work week with their nine-to-five jobs, I too was starting my work week. Except mine would last nine to ten months.

I went to the doctor's private office, and was surprised to see that I was the only one there. I'd thought that "The Anonymous Person" would be there along with her "Uninterested Husband" and quite possibly also her mom. I guess "The Anonymous Person" had better things to do than to be there to see her own baby implanted and fertilized in my womb.

After the implantation, I was put in a hotel where I would stay (with delivered meals and a live-in assistant) until the pregnancy became viable. I was to be checked in two weeks to see if "we were pregnant."

During those two weeks my diet consisted primarily of brown rice, veggies, and fish, fish, fish. I was required to eat so much fish because the doctor said that omega 3's were crucial to the baby's neurological development even from fertilization, so fish is what I ate almost from morning to night.

In two weeks I went back to the doctor's office and was checked. I was not pregnant. Three days from there we redid the fertilization and implantation procedure and I was checked again in two weeks. Again, no pregnancy.

Meanwhile, I had lost eight pounds off my small-medium frame over the course of that month. I knew it was because I hadn't had more than a few grams of fat over the course of the month, and my body was responding. The doctor didn't like that we hadn't gotten pregnant yet, so he increased my caloric intake and allowed a greater variety of foods. And then we tried again.

All in all it took five attempts, or two and a half months to get pregnant. Then, after carrying the baby for only six weeks, I lost it. I hadn't communicated with "The Anonymous Person", but I knew that the doctor was communicating what was going on to them. And I also knew that "The Anonymous Person" and quite possibly even her husband were probably quite disappointed that we had lost the first baby.

It wasn't biologically my own child, but I too was sad and had cried when the doctor confirmed that the bleeding was indeed a miscarriage. We waited a month, during which time I was given a course of hormones that made me sick to my stomach. I had read that six weeks was how long a woman should wait before trying for another baby after a miscarriage, but I knew that "The Anonymous Person" and her husband were on a tight schedule. So we tried again after a month.

When I came back in after the month had passed to retry the fertilization and implantation procedure, the doctor was unusually talkative. He seemed a bit nervous as he spoke somewhat nonstop.

At one point he mentioned a "new shipment from a different source," and some sort of malfunction or dysfunction. He said it so quickly, rambling, that I nearly missed it. Almost as soon as he said it, though, his eyes got very wide and he changed the subject really quickly, which made it catch my attention.

Maybe because of how nervous the doctor appeared or because of his incessant chatting, I got a strange feeling that the new shipment from a different source was new sperm from someone other than the "Uninterested Husband", and that maybe the malfunction or dysfunction was the husband's sperm. I had no way of knowing this for sure, but based on the doctor's strange behavior and the nervousness he had with that day's procedure, as opposed to the previous ones, I got the distinct feeling that "The Anonymous Person" and her "Uninterested Husband" had found out that there was some type of problem with hubby's little swimmers.

I think the doctor's nervousness was because he somehow knew that his job was dependent on getting this done. I think he was running out of time to make this pregnancy happen before "The Anonymous Person" and her "Uninterested Husband" moved on or called the whole thing off.

I wondered if the doctor had been the one to discover the problem with the husband's little swimmers and if he'd had to tell this mega-couple that had achieved record breaking success that they couldn't use his sperm for what would be this couple's (and the world's) super-baby. I had no way of knowing for sure if that was what the doctor meant, but based on what he said, how he said it, and his general nature and nervousness during that time, it made me think that was what he meant.

Also, as I thought about it after the fact, the "Uninterested Husband" was a bit older than his megastar wife and had been in the entertainment industry for quite some time and had never managed to have a child. That seemed a bit odd, and also made me believe that the "new shipment" was indeed different sperm since the husband's weren't up to par. Very briefly, I also wondered where they might've received the "new" sperm. Who could the donor have been? Was it a sperm bank?

I found it all so intriguing, but I knew I couldn't ask the doctor. After he spilled the bit of information he spilled, he clammed up so tight that I could barely get him to speak another word to me.

Sure enough, after two weeks we found out that I was indeed pregnant. The doctor seemed so happy and almost relieved. He checked me again every week until I reached three months of pregnancy. When I reached the second trimester and the doctor thought we were out of harm's way, they then moved me to the secret location to finish the rest of my pregnancy.

When I got to the island and went up to my quarters, there on the table were 12 dozen roses (144 total, I counted them individually) with a little note that said, simply, "Thank you." I knew they were from "The Anonymous Person", and that she was thanking me for carrying her baby. The kind gesture made me smile.

Within two weeks of being there I had already read the novels I had brought with me. Since I couldn't journal or talk on the phone, I was bored to tears. I wasn't even a big phone talker, but at that point I would've talked to a telemarketer just to have something to do.

Although I generally didn't like watching television - probably stemming from my childhood and the fact that we had only had one television, which my dad watched westerns on all the time - I consumed a lot of television in those days.

I had every channel known to man, and total access to any movie I could ever want to see, even some that weren't out yet. I found myself watching all the celebrity gossip shows like TMZ, Inside Edition, and Access Hollywood, so that I could keep up on all my celebrity gossip, and maybe even catch a glimpse of "The Anonymous Person" and her "Uninterested Husband".

It was on one of those shows that I learned that "The Anonymous Person" had finally announced "her" pregnancy. She hadn't announced it on the show itself, but had chosen a place that would have a lot of media to make the announcement there.

I thought that was smart and stupid at the same time. I thought it was smart because the place was such a public venue, that many people (maybe even the whole world) would see it and it would establish a baby timeline. It would be a way of saying, "See, we're pregnant! So expect a baby real soon!" Plus, whoever wasn't tuning in to that particular show could then catch it on any number of shows since there would be so many media sources at such a public place as the one that was chosen to make the "I'm pregnant" announcement.

But I also thought it was the most stupid thing to do because everyone knew that this star is super private, and has maintained privacy in all her personal affairs. So why would she tell the world she was pregnant? She'd never confirmed that she was dating anyone, not even when she and the guy – who later became her husband

- had been dating for many years and spotted around the world together, and everyone knew they were an item.

She hadn't even announced that they'd gotten married even when it was obvious that the world knew, and even after the world knew, she'd never confirmed that they were married - at least not for many years after. So why, just keeping with the way she'd always done things, would she suddenly announce something so private to the entire world?

Again, I understood the need to establish for the world that she was "pregnant," but why not do it in a way that fit with how she and her husband had always done things? So as not to arouse any suspicion?

Although they never asked me, in my opinion, what she did was obvious to anyone with even a little bit of sense. I wondered why her publicist would allow her to make that announcement in that way.

Then I thought about it and reasoned that maybe because having a surrogate was such a private and secret affair she hadn't told her publicist, so her publicist couldn't advise her on how best to establish a pregnancy alibi.

In any case, I felt like anyone with any sense would realize something was off when such a well-established private person announced such a private thing in such a public place, especially when she'd never done anything like that before.

But nobody asked me so I said nothing. I just felt sorry for her. Since I knew she didn't want anyone to find out that she wasn't carrying her own child, I just hoped that she proceeded with more caution in the future. I also had selfish reasons for wanting her to pull this off and maintain my anonymity, because I knew that if anyone found out that I was this person's surrogate, my life would never be mine again.

I knew I wouldn't be able to go anywhere or do anything without being followed by paparazzi and stalked. I did not want the hassle and I did not envy celebrities that had to deal with all that intrusion into their lives. I saw how much celebrities were violated and even their children accosted, and I didn't want that, especially since I wanted to have my own family one day.

I wanted to be able to live a normal, though financially comfortable life, so I wanted "The Anonymous Person" to be a little bit slicker in hiding from the world that she wasn't actually pregnant. But as luck would have it, she would make many more mistakes, and soon the whole world – except for some truly die-hard and willfully stupid fans – would know. Or at least speculate. Little did I know that this was only the beginning.

Now that I knew that she had officially made the announcement, I found myself tuning in to any and every show that provided celebrity information so that I could learn more about her and how she was handling getting ready for this pregnancy. I wanted to know if she knew the sex (after all I was examined every week, so for all I knew the doctor had seen the sex during one of the exams and told her), if she had begun shopping for the baby, what the media was saying about it, and how and if she was dressing and playing the part of a pregnant woman.

After all, it wasn't like she confided in or even had contact with me. As a matter of fact I had tried on more than one occasion to make contact with her but my calls had gone unanswered. I had also left a couple messages for her through the doctor, but they were never met with any responses – meaning she either didn't get the messages or didn't reply. Either way, I obviously had no contact with her.

Several weeks later I tuned in to a show where she was to be interviewed. Before the interview could even start, she had already managed to make the news.

Apparently her pregnancy belly attachment deflated as she went to sit down. I don't know about you, but having been pregnant many times before, I know that a pregnant stomach does not deflate. A pregnant stomach is round and hard. It is definitive. The only molding or moving that it does is much later in the pregnancy when the baby itself starts to protrude, by either pushing out an arm or leg or a butt, or any type of body part.

So again, the celebrity who I had believed to be fairly intelligent had managed to show that she was wearing a pregnancy belly.

Surprisingly, but thankfully, only a small fuss was made about it. I was surprised because I would've assumed pregnant women everywhere would've known that this was a fraud. One only needs to be pregnant or feel a pregnant belly to know the difference. Pregnant stomachs don't deflate or go inward at any point, regardless of how someone is sitting, or what they're wearing.

I gasped when I finally got around to seeing the footage for myself. Then I prepared for the hailstorm. I just knew that "The Anonymous Person" would be busted and that the proverbial poop would hit the fan.

I read the news stories and prepared myself for the worse. But to my surprise it never came. I was astounded to see that people had literally made up stories about what could possibly be the reason her "pregnant" belly so obviously flattened. I heard explanations such as "camera angles," "eyes playing tricks," and even things such as "extra fabric and belly protectors" being accused. Seriously? How stupid were these people?

Although it worked out in my favor, because I would not be outed and exposed to the masses, I began to get upset that so many, especially women who'd been pregnant before, had turned a blind eye to what was so obviously the truth. I came to realize that my anger stemmed from my belief that some people simply preferred being stupid. They'd rather not know. They'd rather be left in the dark.

Case in point, some women didn't want to know if their man was cheating, or they accepted it as long as it was done discreetly (like "Shades'" wife had done). Because after all, according to some, "a man is going to do what a man is going to do." I disagree. A man, a woman, or a dog is going to do what you allow to be done. After all, we teach people how to treat us. So, I was surprised that people seemed to want to play dumb as it pertained to this megastar who was so obviously not pregnant, and had enough blunders for it to show.

Overall, I was growing less and less enchanted with "The Anonymous Person". When we first met she seemed like she was cool, informed, and just an overall good person. It seemed like the charade stopped after I became her employee. She hadn't called once. She hadn't taken my call once. And it wasn't that I became like a stalker, it was just that I was used to the moms (and sometimes even the dads) at least being interested or concerned enough about their impending child to want to check on me and their baby. Some had insisted that I stay with or close to them, many would show up at appointments, and almost all would at least call regularly. The Anonymous Person had done none of that.

"The Anonymous Person" he had left me in the care of her personal doctor and dropped me off as one would their dry cleaning. I didn't know if it was the hormones making me sensitive, or the fact that I had maybe been doing this too long and had grown cynical, but I was beginning to regret the way I was being treated. I looked back at how I had started my surrogacy career – innocently enough, by falling in love with someone, having his child, and letting him adopt the child because he could give her a great home - and now it seemed like I had gotten off track. When had this just become about the money?

I think I was beginning to grow less enchanted with myself as well. I was beginning to think that I was better than I was allowing myself to be treated. It was true that I was making a lot of money, but I was also doing things and accepting behaviors that I knew wouldn't make my parents proud. I think maybe that's why I didn't like to think about them too much, because I knew that if they were looking down on me they wouldn't recognize the daughter they had raised and loved.

This whole thing was making me depressed, so I went to bed. When I awoke the next day I decided that maybe I wouldn't watch so much television or otherwise "spy" on "The Anonymous Person". I told myself that her life was her own and that as long as what she was or wasn't doing wasn't affecting me, that we would have no problems. So far I hadn't been found out, and she had managed to keep up the pregnancy façade, so everything was okay. I reasoned that everything would stay okay as long as they treated me with the respect I felt I deserved.

The third trimester came and went like a breeze. Aside from some tiredness, I was doing really well. I had gotten fairly big, and my breasts were ever-growing (at that point I was a triple D or an F) but thanks to the strict diet the doctor had me on, I had managed to gain all my weight in my belly, as well as in my breasts. As far as "The Anonymous Person", although she had managed to commit several more blunders that any other normal pregnant woman would know better than to do, she had managed to not get herself caught, although speculation was ever-growing.

"The Anonymous Person" had done dumb things like walk around in six and seven inch heels, even though it's a fact that pregnant women lose their equilibrium and balance because of their protruding belly throwing off their center of gravity. She also went to a club one week before I was due to have her baby. Who does that if you're really pregnant? Unless you're a 16 year-old stripper auditioning for the Jerry Springer show, you do not go out clubbing while you are allegedly nine months pregnant.

As weird as it sounds, a small part of me wanted her to get caught. I think it was because I did not want her to think that she was above reproach. But that would've obviously jeopardized my life and career, so at the end of the day I was happy people were blissfully stupid and that she was able to pull off "being pregnant."

Two weeks before I was due "The Anonymous Person" summoned for me to go back to the State where she lived. Although the press hadn't been informed, she had decided that she would deliver there and not in her hometown. I was still being secluded and sequestered, but I was happy to be back in the city and off that island.

Being so close to my due date, I was surprised to see that the doctor hadn't accompanied me back to the city. He had stayed behind to clean up. By "clean up" I'm sure they meant make sure that all signs and proof that I existed was destroyed. I figured this was the case because they wouldn't allow me to take any of my belongings back with me. Not even the pictures of my parents. I was told that the items would be mailed to me at a later date. I think it was because they wanted to go through the items and make sure that I hadn't managed to get my hands on any incriminating evidence.

But I wondered why they didn't realize that someone finding out about this put me at risk too. After all, who would want to work with me as their surrogate if I could no longer ensure anonymity? And if I became known as the face of celebrity surrogacy? The consequence of people finding out about me was that I would be blacklisted. So it was in my best interest that I kept quiet and the couples I surrogate for stayed smart, unless of course, they openly hired a surrogate, and in that case it wouldn't be me because my contract stated that I worked anonymously.

In any case, I was put back at the hotel. Two days later and eight days before I was due, I was called on the phone and told that "The Anonymous Person" wanted to see me. I was taken to the hospital where I would be delivering and told that I would be meeting "The Anonymous Person" there. I wondered why I was meeting her at the hospital, but since this couple had done things so differently than the others, I wasn't too surprised that they'd want to meet there. I just figured that it had something to do with the baby.

A car picked me up in the middle of the night and I was transported to the hospital. Well, when I got there I was whisked away to private quarters. I didn't even know hospitals had those. "The Anonymous Person" and her "Uninterested Husband" had reserved the entire half of the hospital floor. Again, I didn't know that a person could do that. But given the amount of money this couple had at their disposal, I guess I wasn't too surprised.

On the hospital floor was the doctor that had been on the island with me, as well as two nurses, and about a handful of other medical professionals. I briefly wondered why they were all there, but didn't have much time to think because of the excitement of it all. "The Anonymous Person's" mom was also there. And that's when I started to get suspicious and began to wonder what was going on. I didn't have too long to wait before I got the answer to that question.

I was informed by the doctor that they would be taking the baby via Cesarean section the next day. My eyes grew so wide that they nearly fell out of my head. I immediately asked, "Why? Was there something wrong with the baby?"

The doctor looked hesitant to answer me, so I began to ask louder. I guess he didn't want to cause too much of a scene since we were away from the others. Finally he blurted out that I was having the baby via C-section because the "baby's parents" preferred it that way. When I asked why they preferred I have major abdominal surgery to deliver this baby instead of having it the old-fashioned way, he said it was because "The Anonymous Person" preferred that her baby not pass through my vagina.

I was aghast and speechless. It literally took me about five minutes to speak. I just stood there with my mouth wide open, flustered and hyperventilating. I was scared beyond words. I did not want to have surgery and have my stomach cut open to have this baby. What if something happened to me? What if I didn't awake from the surgery? Aside from having a couple wisdom teeth removed many years ago, I had not ever had any type of surgery, and I found myself trembling with fear and trepidation.

I was also highly offended. I was offended that "The Anonymous Person" did not want her child to pass through my vagina. For one thing, this child had spent its entire life inside my body, but now I wasn't good enough to deliver it? And what was wrong with my vagina?

I was so shocked and so hurt that I actually began to cry, even though I'm not normally an emotional person. I demanded to know where "The Anonymous Person" was. I had decided that I was going to confront her about this. That she had gone too far.

I was told that "The Anonymous Person" was in her room getting ready and that I did not have access to her. I yelled, "Getting ready for what?! What exactly is she getting ready for? And what's got her so busy that she can't even take a moment to speak with me?!"

I was ushered into a room where a man in a fancy suit approached me and asked me what was wrong. When I explained to him that I was not comfortable with having a C-section, he whipped out the contract and told me to turn to a certain section. In the section was a clause permitting "The Anonymous Person" complete discretion "with all things pertaining to the birth and raising of the aforementioned child." I had read that, but didn't know that it meant she could determine the birthing and delivery process. Since this was occurring to my body I thought that it pertained to me. And my attorney hadn't indicated anything unusual about that request, so I hadn't thought much about it.

The man in the fancy suit – who I later found out was another one of their attorneys – informed me that the birth of their child and the way they chose to bring the child into the world was a part of that clause. He said if I didn't honor the clause that I would be in violation of the contract and sued. I said, "Well sue me!" because I was under the impression that this high-powered couple would not want this kind of thing to go public.

He again referred me to a section of the contract that said that if things had to go to litigation that we both agree to keep the matter private and to have our cases heard by a closed jury (meaning only a judge) and that if I had reneged on any part of the contract that I would be subject to double the amount I would've been paid in damages. That meant I would've owed them 10 million dollars! So, if I didn't do what they said and have this baby via C-section, that in addition to basically carrying their baby for free, I would also owe them 5 million dollars!

I was flabbergasted and disgusted. But there was nothing I could do. I could refuse and lose all my money, or I could get this surgery over and be done with this couple.

Very angrily I told the attorney that I would do it, but that I wanted nothing else to do with this couple when this was done. I had had enough. I had been disrespected, neglected, treated horribly.

The attorney, instead of sympathizing, told me that the couple also wished to terminate all communication with me after their baby was delivered and final payment was made. And just for good measure, he showed me where in the contract this information was already stated. The statement read, "pursuant to the birth of the child and the acquisition of final payment in the amount of 5 million dollars, all contact between the parties will be terminated and the parties willfully enter into a voluntary agreement to maintain at least 200 yards from each other. This means that neither party will attend events of the other party or communicate in any way. This clause is non-negotiable."

Well, there it was, in black ink. An intelligently written legal statement that essentially said to me that after I had their baby I was to sit down, shut the "f" up, and stay the hell away from them. Hell, I couldn't even attend any of their concerts (which after this I wouldn't have wanted to anyway).

I was so angry at that point that I swore revenge. I decided that I would never be a surrogate for any celebrities ever again, and I made myself a promise that I was going to find a legal way to expose this couple for the frauds that they are.

After I had their baby I was further disrespected by being sequestered in a nondescript hospital room, cared for by their own personal, mean nurse, and then removed from the hospital in the middle of the night like I was a common thief.

Following the surgery it took me several weeks to heal, and a couple more months to feel like myself. Every day I had to look at a line across the bottom of my belly as a reminder that I would get this couple back for the way they treated me. Even though I didn't consider myself a vengeful person, I was going to do something to let them know that what they did was not okay.

In the days, weeks, and months that followed, I saw how they became celebrated. I figured a good way to get back at them would be for the world to see how they really were. I decided that I would tell it all. And that is when *Confessions of a Surrogate for Celebrities* was born.

Chapter 9: The Tell-All

So, I am spilling the beans. Very carefully, spilling the beans. I am simply confirming what most of us thought anyway. I mean, let's keep it real. A week after having a baby you're at a club? As thick as you are before you even get pregnant, you manage to not look pregnant in the first place? No pregnancy mask, no fuller face and/or nose, none of the telltale signs? Then you miraculously lose the baby bump so quickly? The same "baby" bump that had previously deflated?

Some have said that it's because she was a dancer. Well, for one, she dances when she's in concert and not for a living, so her "dancing" is infrequent. And she was already a potato chip away from being a "big girl" before she got "pregnant," so why would she be the same size so shortly after having a baby?

There will always be someone out there who knows someone out there who was the exception. Someone will have a story about how they or a good friend of theirs simply lost the weight right away. My question to them would be: were they as thick as "The Anonymous Person" to begin with? Did their pregnant belly ever simply deflate one day? Did they walk around in six or seven inch heels while "pregnant"?

Performer or not, what would make someone think someone with her size pre-pregnancy wouldn't get thick as hell post pregnancy? People, get real. I don't regret carrying the child for them, because I know that the child will have an incredibly privileged life. And at the end of the day that's what every mother, regardless of her station in life, wants for her child.

What I regret is that I was willing to allow myself to be bought and diminished by others simply because they make more money than me. I will never stoop to that level again.

As for me, I am a full-fledged writer. I have several projects in the works and am excited about my new career. I also have a special someone (who does not yet know that I used to be a celebrity surrogate). I am not planning on telling him, as I do not want to bring my past into my future.

For obvious reasons I have decided to publish this work anonymously, and through a publishing company that specializes in discreetness (TTP Publishing). Many of this publishing house's authors walk among the rich and famous, and now thanks to this publishing house, there is a voice for us.

Be sure to catch my next books, "Open Marriage: An Erotic Trilogy", "Open Marriage: A.S.E. Sports Agency, and "Open Marriage: Behind the Scenes" where I spice up the reading world with a hot and heavy erotic trilogy.

The *Open Marriage Erotic Trilogy* has it all, even some insider knowledge into celebrity sex lives!

PS. Please check out the questions for the Reading Groups, and if you're up for it, join me at www.ttppublishing.com with your responses. See you there!

Questions for Reading Groups:

1. Who do you think the 5 couples are?
2. Would you ever hire a surrogate to carry a child for you? If so, under what circumstances? If not, why?
3. If you hired a surrogate would you keep it a secret? Why or why not?
4. If you hired a surrogate what would you look for in them?
5. Would you rather be a secret/quiet millionaire, or a famous millionaire?

About TTP Publishing

"Providing short and sweet books you can enjoy, when you're ready to enjoy them, that WON'T take all day...

...BECAUSE YOU HAVE THINGS TO DO"

TTP Publishing is a book and media publishing company that specializes in publishing short books. It was founded by an avid reader who, after becoming a mom, doctor, bill-payer, and errand-runner, realized she had little to no time left in a day to sit back and enjoy a good book.

What's more, this busy mom was also impatient, meaning she not only wanted to sit back and enjoy a good book with her limited "me" time, but she also wanted to reach the conclusion of that book - without having to wait days or even weeks before she had more time to read again.

This busy mom had an "aha" moment as she thought of how awesome it would be if good books were shorter and lasted the length of say, a good movie, or dinner out.

That's when **TTP Publishing** - "TTP" stands for **to the point** - was founded.

TTP's books are sometimes funny, sometimes controversial, sometimes spicy, and sometimes tell-it-like-it-is, but they are almost always short and to the point...*because you have things to do.*

For information on submitting your book for publication, please visit us at www.ttppublishing.com, or send us an email to info@ttppublishing.com.

Happy Reading!!!

TTP Publishing Books

*Act Like a CEO, Think Like a Millionaire: Why You Should Care LESS About What a Man or Woman Thinks About Love, Relationships, Intimacy and Commitment and MORE About GETTING WHAT YOU WANT OUT OF LIFE

*What You WON'T Expect When You're Expecting Because This is The CRAP They Don't Tell You: ABC's of a Sucky Pregnancy

*Confessions of a Surrogate for Celebrities

*TESTIMONY: 10 Stories Detailing Supernatural Miracles, Blessings, and THE POWER OF PRAYER

*Open Marriage: An Erotic Trilogy (Book 1)

*Open Marriage: A.S.E. Sports Agency (Book 2)

*Open Marriage: Behind the Scenes (Book 3)